FOR
LUCKY'S SAKE

Avon Books are available at special quantity discounts for bulk
purchases for sales promotions, premiums, fund raising or educa-
tional use. Special books, or book excerpts, can also be created to
fit specific needs.

For details write or telephone the office of the Director of Special
Markets, Avon Books, Dept. FP, 1350 Avenue of the Americas,
New York, New York 10019, 1-800-238-0658.

FOR
LUCKY'S SAKE

PHYLLIS KARAS

AN AVON CAMELOT BOOK

AVON BOOKS
A division of
The Hearst Corporation
1350 Avenue of the Americas
New York, New York 10019

Copyright © 1997 by Phyllis Karas
Published by arrangement with the author
Visit our website at **http://AvonBooks.com**
Library of Congress Catalog Card Number: 96-95262
ISBN: 0-380-78647-8
RL: 4.5

First Avon Camelot Printing: July 1997

CAMELOT TRADEMARK REG. U.S. PAT. OFF. AND IN OTHER COUNTRIES, MARCA REGISTRADA, HECHO EN U.S.A.

Printed in the U.S.A.

OPM   10   9   8   7   6   5   4   3   2   1

For Adam and Josh Karas and their cousins:
Richard Bondy; Charissa and Dana Bondy;
Julie and Beth Karas; and
Sheryl, Kenny, Sam, and Matt Perlow

One

About the last thing I wanted to do that day was take my cousin Elliot to the park. Elliot's five and I'm twelve, and although Elliot most likely couldn't think of anything he'd rather do than go to the park with me, I could think of at least four things I'd rather do. Like skateboard with Peter Chandler or wait for Amelia Parker to deliver our afternoon newspaper. Or lie on the couch and watch *Happy Days* reruns or play NHLPA on my Sega. But Aunt Marcy dropped over to visit Mom, and I just happened to be finishing a peanut butter and cucumber sandwich, and the next thing I knew they were sitting in the kitchen sipping coffee, and Elliot and I were heading to the park.

Truthfully, I don't really mind being with Elliot. Since I'm the youngest in our family and have two older sisters who are identical twins, it's kind of nice to have someone look up to me the way Elliot does. I don't hang around with too many other five-year-olds, but I bet that Elliot is the smartest one around. The kid knows so much he scares me sometimes. Like last week, I was reading a book about the planets for science and Elliot started talking to me about Jupiter and Venus. He knew that Venus was the brightest planet and that Jupiter was the second brightest. Now, that's pretty amazing for a five-year-old. I didn't even know that until he told me. And he can recite the entire alphabet and count to fifty.

Anyhow, Elliot and I spent a good hour at the park, sitting on the seesaw and talking. He'd just rented *The Lion King* the night before and was anxious to talk about it with me. He was real sad about the father lion dying. "It's not like in *Snow White and the Seven Dwarfs*," he explained to me. "The father lion wouldn't wake up if a prince kissed him. He was really, really dead." Elliot looked like he was going to cry, but I got him going on how the movie had been made and he cheered right up. I was in the middle of a description of how animation artists draw tons of pictures to make one short scene when Jimmy Oliver came by. Jimmy and I used to be real good friends last year, but this year, in sixth grade, we hardly see each other. I still think Jimmy's a good kid, but he's changed. He hangs around with some wild kids and if you didn't know him, you'd think he was real tough. He's not, but the way he dresses and combs his hair and talks makes him look that way. We're in a couple of classes together and he hardly ever does his homework or pays attention to the teacher. Still, there's something I like a lot about Jimmy.

At the park, Jimmy was psyched to see Elliot. "Hey, little buddy," he said, sitting down in back of Elliot on the seesaw and shooting me toward the sky with a huge jerking motion. "Let's see if we can send old Benjy for a ride out of here."

Elliot couldn't stop laughing as I jerked around, making a big deal out of trying to get down. The truth was Jimmy weighs a good twenty pounds more than I do and I was pretty well trapped up there. "Hey, Elliot, give me a break!" I yelled down, which set off Elliot even more. He's such a serious little guy that it was great to see him laughing like that.

"What do you think, Elliot old man?" Jimmy asked. "Should we send him a little higher or drop him to the ground like a bag of dirty potatoes?"

"Drop him," Elliot finally eked out, but then his face got serious. "But don't drop him on his head, Jimmy. Auntie Carol will be mad at me if I bring him home broken."

This cracked Jimmy up. When he finally stopped laughing, he let me down. Not like a bag of potatoes, but not like an expensive dish either. "So, how you doing, Benjy?" he asked me after I lifted my body off the ground and settled Elliot in a swing and began to push him. "Did you finish all your math and science homework? Or do you need to copy mine?"

He was trying to be funny. He'd copied my math homework last week. "No thanks," I said. "I think I can manage on my own. How'd you do in track yesterday, anyhow?" One thing Jimmy was great at was long-distance track. He'd actually run in the Boston Marathon last year, as a bandit, tagging along at the end. Jimmy might look like a different person from the one who'd been my friend last year, but his legs had only gotten longer and stronger. "Didn't you have a big meet against Dedham?"

3

Jimmy shrugged his shoulders. "Beats me. I couldn't make it."

I couldn't believe it. Jimmy never missed a meet. "You're kidding," I said. "Weren't you feeling well?"

"No, I was feeling okay. But something came up."

"Oh," I said. "Sure. You going to be running against Newton on Monday?"

"Not sure," he said. "Look, I gotta run. See you later, small fry." He pulled Elliot and his swing way back, held on to them for a good, long minute, and then sent the swing flying higher into the air than I'd been able to manage. Elliot's delighted whoop could be heard for miles. And then Jimmy was gone. Leaving me baffled.

"Jimmy looks different," Elliot said as we walked back to my house. "Did he join a gang or something?"

"No, he didn't join a gang or anything," I said. "He just wears his hair different now. That's all."

"And he wears all-black clothes. I'd like to wear all-black clothes and spike my hair like his."

"You're only five, Elliot," I reminded him. "You'll have to wait a few years till you change your hair and clothes."

"Will Jenny and Jillian be home when we get to your house?" he asked.

"Probably," I said. "Why? Would you rather hang out with them than me?"

"No," he answered very seriously. "I like you a thousand times better. But they promised they'd bake brownies next time I came over and I'm in the mood for a real chocolaty brownie. With lots of nuts."

"I thought you were allergic to nuts," I said.

4

"I'm back on nuts," he said. "I'm off carrots and orange juice, but back on nuts and milk."

"That whole allergy stuff can be so confusing," I said. "I don't know how they figure it all out."

Elliot was just completing his explanation of injecting a patient's arm or hand or back or leg with particles of each substance and watching how the skin reacts when we reached my house. I couldn't have been more relieved. I have a real thing about needles and Elliot's description of the needles he'd had to endure the day before was turning my stomach upside down. The kid was in luck. Both my sisters were in the kitchen, whipping up a batch of brownies for their favorite cousin. It's funny. Jenny and Jillian are identical fifteen-year-old twins and just about everybody has a terrible time telling them apart. I mean, I've lived with them for twelve years and occasionally I get them mixed up. They don't dress alike, but their hair is the same length and they weigh the same exact amount, and their features and voices are absolutely identical, so it's natural that it takes everyone a minute to figure out who's who. But not Elliot. Immediately, he knew that Jillian was mixing the batter and Jenny was greasing the brownie pan. And that was two more things than I knew.

My sisters both adore Elliot. If they were one hundredth as nice to me as they are to our little cousin, I'd be grateful. Me, they yell at all the time. There's practically nothing I can do that makes them happy. It wouldn't be so bad if there were just one of them, but there's two. And they never get mad at each other. My dad tells me to ignore them and go about my business. He tells me I have to like myself more than I need anyone else to like me. But my dad is a psychiatrist and is always saying things like that. My mom insists that my sisters love me and they're just going through a stage where it seems as if they hate me. The truth is neither one of my parents understand what it's like having two sisters that everyone thinks are the two cutest things on the face of the earth. If I had a quarter for every guy who got all nutso when he heard who my sisters were, I'd be a rich man. But I'm not. Instead, I'm the poor little brother who gets treated like garbage by two beauties.

Elliot was getting the royal treatment from both princesses. Jillian was letting him lick the spoon, and Jennifer was handing him more chocolate chips than she was putting in the batter. The minute I came near the batter, both my sisters had hissy fits. "Don't you dare put your dirty hands in there!" Jillian shrieked.

"Don't you have some homework to do?" Jennifer asked when I ignored Witch No. 1 and spooned myself a big glob of their precious batter. "I mean, maybe if you did five minutes a night, you might be able to pass one class in sixth grade. I hate to think what's going to happen to you next year when you hit junior high. You know, your grades do count now."

"Really?" I asked. "I thought I was still in play group. But don't worry. Now that I understand where I am, somehow I'll manage to surpass your brilliant performance in math class." That was a low blow. Jenny was having a terrible time in ninth grade geometry. She'd actually flunked a quiz last week. Mom was frantic and had already sent her to a math tutor twice.

But Jenny didn't have to defend her honor against me. Jillian wiped me out in one single swoop. "So how

6

did you do at basketball tryouts?'' she asked in her fake sweet voice. She knew I was dying to make the team and that my chances were one in a million. The sixth-grade class had an awesome group of basketball players. Mr. Murray, the coach, said he'd never had a group like this before. He'd already announced there would be lots of kids who wouldn't make the team. But so far he hadn't cut anyone. I'd done terrible at yesterday's try-outs and was sure that after tomorrow's tryout I'd be the first cut. It was too bad because I wasn't a bad player. I had a great three-pointer and some fancy plays under the hoop, but my footwork wasn't fast enough to keep up with the rest of the kids. The fact that I was the shortest kid trying out didn't help either.

I was thinking of a great retort for Jillian, maybe something about the tiny pimple forming over her right lip, when Mom and Aunt Marcy came in. Aunt Marcy wrapped her arms around Elliot and gave him this giant hug. Since he was busy mixing the batter at that moment, it wasn't the perfect time for a hug, but Elliot held on to his spoon and was still in one piece when she finally let him go.

Then she walked over to me and gave me a pretty solid squeeze. I hate it when anyone hugs me, but Aunt Marcy's different. She's just so much fun. She's the biggest *Simpsons* fan in the world and always invites us all over to her house every Sunday evening for a Simpson party. She cooks up her special Simpsonburgers, loaded with bacon and mayonnaise and everything fatty that Homer loves, puts on her blue Marge wig, which stands about four feet high in the air, and talks in a Marge grunt. Even Uncle Bobby, who could care less about *The Simpsons,* cracks up over her. Aunt

7

Marcy gets everybody, even my mom, into the Simpson mood. I don't think I could watch that show with anyone besides her. "How you doing, Bartie old boy?" she asked me in her gravely Marge voice. "Did you have fun at the park or was it totally boring?"

"Aw, I survived," I said in my Bart voice, which I have to admit is a pretty good imitation. "But tomorrow I'm off to the studio to see Crusty the Clown. No stopping me from that."

Aunt Marcy laughed and I swear even my two hideous sisters did, too. Then a funny thing happened. Aunt Marcy started to cry. I've never seen her cry in my whole life. Not that I've seen a lot of women cry in my whole life. I saw my mother cry a couple of months ago when I broke her favorite vase when I was roughhousing with Peter. Man, that was not a pretty sight. And she cried at Papa's funeral. But that was about it for crying from my mom. Seeing Aunt Marcy cry was a horrible thing. Even Jillian and Jennifer looked shocked. Elliot's mouth opened real wide and the next thing I knew, he was crying too. Mom was the only one in the kitchen who was able to move. She scooped up Elliot, put her arms around her sister, and led the two of them out of the room.

"Man, what's happening?" I asked my sisters, expecting some insult about my low level of intelligence, but instead they both just shrugged and stared at me like they were as lost as I was. The strangest thing was that their four identical blue eyes weren't filled with the usual revulsion I see when they look at me. All I could see was sadness and confusion. I can't think of anything that upset me more than their reactions.

The next morning my mother didn't leave for work

until after the three of us left for school. That's pretty unusual. She runs an animal shelter that promises never to put an animal to sleep and the morning is always a busy time for her. Lately, there have been a lot of animals dropped off at the shelter during the night and my mom likes to be the first one to find them in the morning. She says that's when they need the most attention. I know the real reason she likes to be there is that she's afraid some of the animals might be dead and she doesn't want the rest of her staff to find them. Everyone says her shelter is a miracle, that she manages to find homes for animals like no one else in the world can. But I think the fact that she can leave our house every day and arrive at work, not knowing what's going to be sitting in a basket outside the shelter's front door, is beyond amazing.

That morning she looked tired, like she hadn't slept at all the night before. She hadn't had supper with us that night, either. She'd had to go to some big meeting at her shelter, so I hadn't had a chance to ask her what was going on with Aunt Marcy. Dad had worked late, and the twins had heated up some leftover spaghetti for me and then eaten cereal in their rooms. They're always on diets, and whenever Mom and Dad aren't around they eat nothing but cereal. The twins had already left for school and Dad had gone to make rounds at the hospital, so it was just me and Mom. "What's up with Aunt Marcy?" I asked while she was gulping down her own bowl of cereal. "She seemed real upset about something yesterday."

Mom looked up at me and shook her head. Man, did she look tired. "She has a serious problem, Benjy," she said. "But I'm hoping everything's going to work out all right."

I felt my stomach sink. "Is she sick?" I asked. I'd watched a sad television show where the father got sick and was dying. I could just imagine Aunt Marcy lying in a hospital bed, breathing her last breath. "You've got to tell me, Mom. Is it her heart?"

My mom sighed and put down her spoon. "It's not her heart, Benjy," she said. "She has a lump in her breast and the doctors think it might be cancerous. She's having a biopsy tomorrow and we're all nervous about it, but we have to hope that maybe they're all wrong."

I couldn't believe what my mother was telling me. I'd heard plenty about cancer in the past year. Johnny Simon's grandmother had died from lung cancer last year and Carly Curtis's father had to keep going into the hospital for treatment because of some kind of cancer in his liver. "Wow," I said. "This is real serious."

"Well, we're not sure exactly how serious, honey," she said. "We'll know tomorrow. We just have to try and be brave until we know exactly what's going on."

"Poor Elliot," I said.

"Oh, he'll be fine," my mother said. "Uncle Bob is going to bring him over here before he takes Marcy to the hospital. I'll get him ready for kindergarten and he'll spend the night here. He's so crazy about you, he won't miss his mom one bit. Look, Benjy, I'm sorry I had to tell you this before school. I really wanted to wait till tonight, after dinner. But you have to remember we don't even know if she has cancer. Try not to worry too much."

There was no doubt my mother wasn't taking her

10

own advice, but I promised I would. When Peter Chandler arrived at our house, I felt like crying. That's pretty gross for a twelve-year-old boy to admit, but that's how I felt. Luckily, Peter was carrying on about basketball tryouts and didn't even notice that I was in such bad shape.

"I think you've got a good shot, Benjy," he told me as we walked to school. "If you could just get in a couple of threes during tryouts, you'd have a good chance. I'll try to feed you anytime I can. I was so bad yesterday, I think I'm done in."

Peter was at least three inches taller than me and played great defense. I was positive he'd make the team. We'd been best friends since we were little kids and had spent thousands of hours at each other's basketball nets, shooting hoops. Peter had just grown taller than me this past summer. He'd also grown something that made the girls notice him. I couldn't figure out what it was. Sometimes when we were with girls, they'd act silly around him. The twins said Peter was turning into a hunk. Of course, they also said I was turning into a worse geek than I'd been in fifth grade. You'd think with two older sisters I might have some understanding of what makes girls tick, but the truth was my knowledge on that subject was a big, fat zero. Still, despite the confusing world of girls, it was a lot worse to think Peter might be on the sixth-grade basketball team, and I wouldn't be. "You're going to make it, Peter," I told him. "I saw the coach write something down after you held off Brian Kelly yesterday."

"I don't know, Benjy. I just don't know."

It was funny. Basketball was the most important thing in the world to me. It even meant more to me than

Amelia Parker and I thought she was pretty, but I got this weird feeling that what was going on with Aunt Marcy was a lot more important than whether or not I made the hoop team. It didn't make me feel good to be thinking like that. As a matter of fact, it made me feel even worse than I already did. I've always been big on making special bargains with God, so I made one while Peter was talking about basketball tryouts. If Aunt Marcy could be okay and not have cancer, I'd give up my spot on the basketball team.

"Okay, God," I said to myself while my best friend recounted my key shots two days earlier. "That's it. Let Aunt Marcy be okay and I'll give up my spot." It seemed like a pretty fair bargain. I mean, that was a pretty huge sacrifice on my part. I just hoped God would agree.

Two

Amelia Parker was standing by my seat when Peter and I walked into homeroom. Last year she went to a different elementary school than Peter and me, but she'd been my paper girl for over a year. She's pretty, with long blond hair and these big black eyes. It used to be great when she'd collect at our house every Friday afternoon, but for the past few months we've been getting a bill sent to our house and my mom just mails in the money. So, the only way I get to see her is when she drops off the paper from her bike every afternoon between four-thirty and five. "Hi, Benjy," she said when she saw me in homeroom. It was sort of exciting that she knew my name. We'd never really talked before. She always said thanks when I used to hand her the newspaper money, but she'd never spoken to me in school. "I need to ask you something."

Peter gave me a little poke in the ribs, which was a good thing to do since I had a hard time opening my mouth and answering Amelia. "Oh, yeah?" I answered, real intelligent like. "What?"

She looked at me with those dark black eyes and I was positive I wouldn't be able to speak another word. "It's about your mother," she said. "She owns that animal shelter down on Western Avenue, doesn't she? The one that promises never to put an animal to sleep."

"Yeah," I answered and I was grateful I got that much out. It was all so weird. I mean, Amelia is not the first girl I have ever spoken to in my life. I'm good friends with Wendy Brown and Jessica Francis. Peter and I go to the movies with them lots and the four of us play basketball or baseball together or go for bike rides. But this Amelia was something different. She was just so pretty that she made it hard for me to breathe around her. I looked up at Peter and he looked as calm and normal as if we were talking to Wendy and Jessica.

Amelia leaned against my desk and stared at me hard. Then she bit her bottom lip and looked unbelievably sad. "I need to speak to your mom about my dog, Boo Boo. He's a lhasa apso and . . . " She stopped and lowered her eyes to the floor. Then there was this huge silence and Peter looked at me, and I shrugged my shoulders, and no one said anything for what felt like two years, but was probably about a minute.

"So what happened to Boo Boo?" Peter asked, and I was so grateful to him I wanted to hug him, which just shows how nutty this girl was making me.

Amelia looked up at Peter like she'd never seen him before, which is ridiculous since he's always sitting on my front steps with me when I wait to watch her throw our paper onto the steps. Amelia gave Peter a little smile and took a deep breath. "Boo Boo bit my cousin Richard this weekend,'' she told him, her voice softer than before. ''My father went crazy. He said we have to get rid of Boo Boo. To put him to sleep.'' I could see the tears in the corners of her black eyes.

''Wow,'' Peter said. ''Just 'cause he bit one person?''

''Well, Richard isn't the first person he's bitten. He's bitten a few others, but they've always been like little nibbles. You know, like when someone he didn't know surprised him by trying to pat him. Or touched his tail. He's real sensitive about his tail. Or if someone was making a lot of noise or jumping around and startled him. But this was the first time Boo Boo really broke someone's skin. My father says you can't keep a dog that bites.''

''How old is Boo Boo?'' Peter asked. I was going to ask the same question but my mouth was tied shut with invisible tape and would most likely never open again.

''Three,'' Amelia answered. She was staring at Peter real hard. Then she looked at me, the silent stupid one. ''Do you think your mom will take Boo Boo to her shelter?''

I nodded. The truth is my mom has a policy about dogs that bite. She will not give them to families with children and has a hard time finding them homes. She spends a long time analyzing each situation involving a biter. Sometimes, she won't take the dog at all and recommends that it be put to sleep. She always says that deciding what to do with biters is one of the hardest parts of her job. But that didn't matter. This was Amelia Parker we were talking about. Amelia, who knew my name. Amelia, who was staring at me as if she were waiting for an answer. ''Yup,'' I finally answered.

When it was apparent that the invisible tape had now

snapped my lips shut again, Peter returned to my rescue. "Mrs. Morgan's the greatest for saving dogs' lives," he said. "You just bring Boo Boo to the shelter this weekend." He looked at me and I blinked my eyes twice. That's what people in comas do when they want to say yes. By some miracle, Peter understood coma talk. "Benjy and I are there every Saturday all day. You bring Boo Boo in and we'll take care of him."

"Oh, thank you so much," Amelia said, fixing those black eyes on Peter. It took a minute but she got them off Peter and onto me, the mute one. "I really appreciate it, Benjy. Boo Boo and I will see you Saturday morning."

After Amelia had left our homeroom, I sank into my seat, exhausted. "What's the matter with you?" Peter asked.

The invisible tape was still in place around my lips. I shrugged my shoulders and took out my vocabulary words. Mr. Orlen was going to give us a quiz in English and I hadn't spent two seconds memorizing the words. It was time to see if my brain was working even if my mouth wasn't.

Wendy Brown and Jessica Francis ate lunch with me and Peter and Johnny Simon. Wendy was eating celery sticks and a carrot and an apple, and Jessica was eating a tuna fish sandwich she'd brought from home. The cafeteria was introducing healthy foods this week, and Peter, Johnny, and I had a few weird things on our tray that not one of us could identify. "I thinks that's guacamole," Johnny said, pointing to the green blob that sat on top of my chicken taco.

"And that's definitely tofu," Peter said as he speared a disgusting white cube the consistency of jello from

16

his salad. "All I know is it's high in protein or something and my mother puts it in everything she cooks that doesn't have meat in it." It stayed in his mouth for less than two seconds. "Oh, my God!" he yelled as he spit it back onto his tray. "I guess, you can't eat it raw. It's life-threatening this way."

"Want a carrot?" Wendy asked. "I think you're safe with something crunchy and orange."

"Is that all you're eating?" I asked. "Are you on another diet?"

"No, I'm not on another diet," Wendy answered, looking real insulted. "I'm on a lifetime pattern of good health. Diets don't do any good. You just gain back whatever you lost the minute you go off the diet. I'm changing my eating habits so I can be thin forever."

Never would I be able to figure out girls' eating habits. The twins were always on diets. Yet they pigged out late at night when they were watching TV or sitting around with their friends during the weekend. It was like they never ate normal. Either they starved or pigged out. Nothing in between. Yet they always looked the same. The twins, Wendy, and Jessica. Guys were so much easier to understand. We ate what we wanted when we were hungry and didn't eat what we didn't want when we weren't.

"I saw Amelia Parker talking to you in homeroom," Jessica said, munching on potato chips. "What was that all about?"

"Nothing much," I said real casually, only I nearly choked on my taco when Jessica said the name Amelia. Still, choking was better than stunned silence. "She needed to ask me a question about my mom's shelter. She's going to bring her dog over. It's a biter."

17

"Your mom hates biters," Johnny said. "Remember that German shepherd that bit the postman? She wouldn't keep it."

"That dog bit the postman every day for two years," I reminded him. "Plus he weighed one hundred pounds. That's different than a fifteen-pound lhasa. My mom will handle this one."

"I hope so," Wendy said in a real funny voice. "I'd hate to see Amelia unhappy."

I looked at Wendy carefully. She looked different since sixth grade started. Up till now, I wasn't sure what it was, but after staring at Amelia that morning, I had figured it out. Wendy was wearing makeup. Not a lot. Just some stuff around her eyes and lipstick. Like Amelia. Only Wendy's eyes were nothing like Amelia's. Wendy's hair was different this year, too. She'd always worn it in braids. Now, it kind of fell over her shoulders. It wasn't blond like Amelia's but it was kind of a neat shade of reddish brown. It was weird to think about Wendy like that. I mean, we'd been good friends since kindergarten. Still, there was no doubt she'd changed since last year. The twins said she was going to be a knockout someday. I suppose they would know about that since everybody but me thought they were knock-outs. Still, Wendy was Wendy. She was no Amelia.

"So, is she bringing her dog to the shelter?" Jessica asked.

"Yeah," I answered. "On Saturday."

"Good. We'll all get a chance to see who it bites," Wendy answered.

I remembered that all five of us always help my mom out on Saturdays, her busiest day. Somehow, the thought of Amelia walking in with Boo Boo and seeing the five of us wasn't my idea of how I wanted to show Amelia around the shelter. I wasn't even sure I wanted Johnny around, never mind Wendy and Jessica. I wasn't dying to have Peter there either, but since I was a mute around Amelia, it made good sense to have someone present who could interpret my blinks. "Yeah," I said, wondering if I could ever come up with a reason why just Peter and I had to be there alone with my mom on Saturday. Maybe I could invent some sort of a rare virus that could be spread to humans. I would tell the other three that even though Peter and I had been able to be immunized, there wasn't enough of the vaccine to go around. It wasn't perfect, but maybe I could work along those lines. Wendy wouldn't be easy to deal with, but I was determined to give it a good try.

Basketball practice was a disaster. Everywhere I moved, the ball didn't. And everywhere the ball moved, I wasn't. Johnny, who was even worse than me, decided to drop out of the tryouts. So I was, without question, the weakest player on the floor. I was tempted to just walk off the court and spare Mr. Murray the trouble of cutting me, but Jillian and Jenny were in the gym, since the ninth-grade cheerleaders use part of our gym for their practices, and it would have been too mortifying to have them see me leave before tryouts ended.

Just my luck their practice ended before our tryouts and they came over to watch the end of my disaster. The only good thing was that every guy trying out, except Peter and me, kept staring at them, and I was able to get my hands on the ball for the only time all afternoon. Peter fed me two good opportunities and I landed two three-pointers.

19

"Atta boy, Benjy!" the twins both shouted when I landed my second three-pointer. It's amazing. The two of them hate me to pieces, but when we're around other people, they can be so nice I almost lose my mind and begin to wonder if I'm imagining how they torture me at home. "Way to go, Benjy!"

Will Sheridan, a junior whom Mr. Murray had made an assistant coach, gave my sisters a real big smile and nearly fell over a ball when they both smiled back at him. They gave him two real sweet waves, blew me a kiss, and took off. No one said anything for a few seconds, so Peter and I just kept throwing the ball around. Personally, I think Amelia's a thousand times prettier than my sisters, but I doubt that anyone on that basketball court would agree with me. "How'd you get so lucky to get a personal cheer from those two cheerleaders?" Will asked me when Jenny and Jillian were no longer in view and he could look back toward the basket.

"They're my sisters," I said.

"No kidding," he said and stared at me for a long minute.

"Okay, guys," Mr. Murray said, "that'll do it. I'll have the list up outside the gym by the end of school tomorrow. Thanks for coming. You're all real good. I just wish I could take you all, but I can't."

Peter and I walked home real slowly. I'd already missed Amelia, and I wasn't anxious to begin the long wait till tomorrow afternoon. "I guess I really blew it today," I said when we got to Peter's house.

"You were a little stronger yesterday," Peter admitted. "But you got good at the end today."

"Yeah, I was great when the coach wasn't looking

at me," I said. "I'm gone. But you're in. You were solid every day of tryouts."

Peter shrugged and walked toward his house. "See you tomorrow," he said. As I walked toward my house, I suddenly remembered the bargain I'd made with God. I'd give up the team for Aunt Marcy not to have cancer. Maybe that was why I had done so terrible. It was all part of God's plan. Okay, I decided, feeling a little better about the whole thing. That explains it. It was all out of my hands.

Three

Aunt Marcy's surgery got scheduled real early the next morning, so Elliot slept over that night. No matter how the twins and I tried to cheer him up, nothing worked. The twins baked him chocolate cupcakes, but he didn't even want to lick the batter off the bowl. My father started in with his magic tricks, which Elliot usually loves, but Elliot looked bored during his entire performance. Even when my dad pulled the nickel out of Elliot's ear and turned a black-and-red circle into a yellow-and-green triangle. "Be a good listener if he needs to talk," my dad told me when Elliot got ready for bed and asked me to read him a story. "Don't push him. When he's ready to talk, he'll talk." Truthfully, I didn't need a shrink to tell me that.

I read Elliot a chapter from his favorite book, *The Little Prince,* and he looked like he was asleep before the last page. There's something about that little prince, the way he looks so serious and unique, with his blond curls and long robe, that reminds me of Elliot. We rented *The Little Prince* movie once, and I swear I was practically in tears when the snake bit the little prince. Elliot actually took it better than me. "He's going back to his planet," he consoled me at the end. "He'll be back with his rose." Just as I was about to leave the room, Elliot opened his eyes. "Do you think my mother has cancer?" he asked me as I edged toward the door.

Now that was a question I could have used a little psychiatric advice about answering. But since I was all on my own, I took a deep breath and said, "I don't know."

"She says even if she has cancer, she will only have a little bit of it."

"Oh, that's real good," I said, coming back to sit on the edge of his bed. It's amazing. I know the kid is only five, but he sounds fifty. "I know if they catch cancer early, they can cure it."

"If she dies, I'd like to live with you," he said, and I just about fell off the bed. "Me and my dad could move in here, don't you think?"

Just when I think Elliot has said the most amazing thing in the world, he comes out with something like this. "That sounds good," I said, trying to imagine what my dad would have said to that one. He probably would have begun a long discussion about why Elliot thought that would be such a good idea. That's my dad's specialty. Asking questions that are supposed to make you answer your own questions. Maybe in his office that works, but in our house it never does. Still, I wouldn't have minded having him on the bed beside me at that moment. "But I really don't think she's going to die, Elliot. Honest."

Elliot looked up at me, real serious, and then closed his eyes. "Night, Benjy," he said, and he turned over and buried his face in the pillow. Man, did he look small in that bed, lying on his stomach, his face lost in the pillow.

"Night, Elliot," I said, and I leaned over and kissed the top of his head. I'm not into kissing at all, but there was no way I could walk out of that room without doing that. My mother was on the phone, talking to Ellen, the lady who runs a farm where my mom sends the greyhounds that she manages to rescue from the racetrack. Bluehound Track is in Livingston, the town next to ours, and is a popular place with the local residents. I can't think of too many things my mother hates as much as she hates that track. I think if she ever found out that I went to that track, she'd throw my bed and clothes onto the lawn. She says that the way they treat greyhounds at the tracks is the worst example of cruelty to animals she's ever seen.

Until she found Ellen, my mom was always bringing former racing greyhounds to her shelter. Sometimes, she'd have as many as ten greyhounds at a time there and would have to bring a few to our house. Now my mom takes all the greyhounds she rescues to Ellen's farm in New Hampshire. Ellen runs this special organization called Adopt-a-Greyhound that finds homes just for greyhounds. Ellen loves greyhounds even more than my mom does, and she'll come down in the middle of the night if my mom calls her and tells her she has a new greyhound.

I was pretty shocked the first time my mother told me about the way they treat greyhounds at the track. She says the greyhounds are muzzled all day long. They live in iron cages which are stacked one on top of the other in tight enclosed spaces. They are let out of these cages just three times a day. The muzzle comes off only when they eat. That's the only time their teeth or tongues are free to lick a paw or bite an itch. Except for a few greyhounds with lightning speed who run until they die, the other greyhounds are gassed to death or shot or put in decompression chambers. It's the most awful story you could imagine, but there's no sense in pretending it doesn't happen every day at the track. And it gets even worse. The greyhounds who aren't killed are sold to labs. The fact that they're very gentle and well behaved makes them perfect for these experiments. It's just awful for all the greyhounds who end up at the track. Whether they are raced to death or put to sleep or sold to labs, unlike the bettors at the track, they just never win.

Anyhow, Ellen takes all the greyhounds my mother can get her hands on and gets them spayed and given the necessary tests. Then, for one hundred fifty dollars, someone can adopt the greyhound. They make the best pets imaginable. They are so quiet and gentle and hardly bark at all. Since they've been raised with other dogs, they get along great with other family pets. It doesn't take long at all to deprogram them from chasing. They're also great with little kids and will walk away from an annoying child rather than snap at him. Even if the kid is pulling its tail or poking it in the eye. Believe me, I've seen the way some kids act around them, and these greyhounds never bite. The only thing you have to be careful of is not to put them on a run, because they might run to the end of it and choke themselves rather than stop. That's because they're so programmed to race. I can't help it. I just love the greyhounds. More than any other animal I've ever seen. They're just so sensitive and lovable. And smart.

That night, my mom was spending the whole night talking to Ellen. "I don't know what I'd do without that woman," she told me when she finally hung up and came into the kitchen where I was eating one of the cupcakes Benjy had refused. "I've got seven greyhounds coming in tomorrow and Ellen could care less. She's got room for all of them."

Ellen is an amazing woman. She's huge, like well over two hundred pounds and close to six feet tall, and always has this incredible energy. People often say that dogs look like their owners. There was nothing about Ellen that looked like a greyhound. She should have collected bull mastiffs. "Is she coming down tomorrow to get them?" I asked as I licked the frosting off a cupcake that had Elliot written on it.

"That's the problem," my mom said. "She's got a big happening with her Adopt-a-Greyhound organization over the next few days. Unfortunately, I'm mobbed at the shelter. I may have to bring a few home tomorrow. Then I'll bring the dogs up to Ellen myself on Saturday. It's the least I can do for her. With Aunt Marcy in the hospital, it's not the greatest time for me to be doing this, but what choice do I have?"

My mom does this a lot. She talks to herself. It wouldn't do any good if I answered her question. She wouldn't hear me. So I just continued to eat the cupcakes. I did want to ask her about Boo Boo Parker, but I sensed this was not a good time to bring up a lhasa that bit. Especially if she was going to be heading up to New Hampshire on Saturday, the day Boo Boo was coming in to have his life saved. "I'll just have to see if Sheryl or Allison can take a couple till Saturday. We'll just have to do the best we can, right?" I nodded. She sank down in the chair beside me and grabbed a cupcake and ate it in about two seconds. "Poor Elliot," my mom said after she poured us each a glass of milk. "He's a wreck about his mother."

"He asked me if she had cancer," I told her. "Do you think she does?"

She shook her head and emptied her glass before I'd finished a third of mine. "I'm worried, Benjy. The doctor wanted that lump out right away. It's strange, though. We have no history of breast cancer in our family. And Aunt Marcy is so careful about what she eats. I'm the one with the lousy eating habits, not her. I swear, once this whole thing is over, I've got to get myself into a better eating regimen. And I've got to get my breasts checked."

Man, did I feel funny hearing my mother talk about her breasts. I could feel the red spreading all over my face. I finished my milk quickly. "So, when will her operation be over?" I asked while my mother studied the front of her sweater.

"They're doing the biopsy at seven-thirty," she told me. "Aunt Marcy decided that if it is cancer, she'll have the lumpectomy right then. They send the tissue from the biopsy to the lab and know right then and there. Well, they don't know everything, but they do have a good idea if it's benign or malignant. Thank heavens Grandma Evelyn is in California. Can you imagine if she were here now?"

I could imagine it well. Grandma Evelyn worries about everything that doesn't happen. If she knew one of her two daughters was having an operation for cancer, they'd have to put her out till after the surgery was over. "Can I call you at the hospital and find out what's happening?" I asked.

"I don't know how you can reach me there," she said. "But I promise to call Dad and you can call his office and speak to him, probably sometime after ten o'clock. Okay?" I nodded and she looked at me hard. "Hey, aren't you in the midst of basketball tryouts? The twins said they saw you trying out today. How's it going?"

"I stunk up the court," I told her. "I'll never make the team. I'm too short and too lousy."

"That's ridiculous," she said. "You're terrific. And don't worry. If you don't make the basketball team, you can always work on the newspaper. You write so well, Benjy. Believe me, that will look much better on a college application."

My mom was a freak with this college stuff. I was in sixth grade and she was already worrying about getting me into Harvard. "I'm not working on the newspaper," I told her. "They already had a meeting and I didn't go. If I don't make the basketball team, I'll have to come home and watch television by myself every day after school. I'll have no one to hang out with either. Because Peter will definitely make the team."

"Oh God, Benjy," she moaned, "I simply can not find time to worry about you tonight. Between Aunt Marcy and Elliot and the greyhounds and the twins, I don't have one spare second to fit you into my worrying schedule." She stood up and carried our glasses to the sink and immediately rinsed them out. "You're on your own with this one, kid."

28

"What's the matter with the twins?" I asked, my ears immediately perking up with the thought of something bad happening to them.

"Oh, nothing you need to bother yourself about," she told me, shaking her head worriedly, and I felt better by the second. "Just get your homework done and grow a few feet tonight so you can make the basketball team and spare us all a lot of grief." Then the phone rang and it was Ellen again. I decided to finish my math homework and leave the growing and the everything else to someone else I'd already declared in charge of my life. Man, this direct line to God was coming in handy these days.

Four

Amelia Parker was waiting by my seat in homeroom again. "Hi," she said to me, barely looking at Peter. "I'm sorry to be such a pain, but I wondered if you'd had a chance to speak to your mom about Boo Boo." When I looked at her with the blank look that she was fast coming to realize was my permanent state of idiocy, she went on. "It's just that my dad is real serious about getting rid of Boo Boo. He picked up my mother's pocketbook to move it from a kitchen chair before dinner and Boo Boo snapped at him. He didn't bite him, but it was a pretty scary snap. My dad got so upset. He said he's calling the vet today and having Boo Boo put to sleep before he really hurts someone. I know he won't do anything till this weekend, because he's going on a business trip today, but he's real serious about it. I just have to be sure it's really okay if I bring Boo Boo to the shelter on Saturday."

I shook my head, which was a pretty big deal for a

comatose person to do. Unfortunately, anyone seeing that shake would have a hard time figuring out what it meant. It could have meant, "Too bad, but that dog is doomed," or, "I'll make sure that dog is saved," or, "I have no idea what's going to happen to that dog." Amelia kept looking at me, hoping for a sign that Boo Boo was going to live past Saturday, but there was no way I could get the invisible tape off my mouth.

"So, she should bring the dog over to the shelter Saturday morning, right, Benjy?" Peter said. He looked weird. Not as weird as me. But weird. Almost like he wanted to laugh. But he's a good friend and he didn't laugh. Instead, he just talked as if it were no big deal to talk when Amelia Parker's sleeve was touching my sleeve and I could smell this perfume like it was a giant flower pressing against my nose.

"Thanks, Benjy," Amelia said when Peter finished talking. "I'll see you Saturday, real early." And then she was gone, leaving this faint whiff of some flower I certainly couldn't name. Then I started to wonder if maybe when you can't speak, your other senses get real strong. Maybe mutes have incredible senses of smell. "Did you smell that?" I asked Peter once Amelia had vanished.

"Smell what?" he asked, still looking at me real weird.

"Amelia's perfume. I swear she wasn't wearing any perfume yesterday. Man, is that a powerful smell. What do you think it is?"

Now it was Peter's turn to shake his head. Only there wasn't any question what his shake meant. It meant, "You're nuts, Benjy. Totally nuts."

Luckily, however, Peter didn't have a chance to express his shake because Johnny came in and told us the coach was putting up the basketball list in five minutes. Peter started to race out the door and I tried to follow but my legs had turned to rubber. Between Amelia and basketball, I was a mere shadow of the once active, speaking human being I had previously been. By the time I got there, Coach was taping the typewritten list to the gymnasium door. Before I had a chance to decompose a little bit more, Peter was thumping me on the back. "We both made it, Benjy!" he was shouting. "Both of us!"

"Nice going, guys," Johnny was telling us while I stood there, my mouth open, doing some more of my now famous head shakes. "I wish I'd tried out, too."

I knew it was a minor miracle that I'd made the team, but it would have been a miracle like the parting of the Red Sea if Johnny had made it. He's a great kid and a lot of fun, but he's so uncoordinated, he makes me look like a total jock. My dad says his problem is bad eye-hand coordination. I'm not sure about that, but whatever it is, it keeps Johnny on the sidelines, where I was convinced I should have been.

I wanted to be happy that I'd made the team and I was, but it wasn't just my feelings about Johnny that were worrying me. I remembered the pact I'd made with God. I'd said I'd give up the team if Aunt Marcy didn't have cancer. Did this mean she had cancer? I looked at the clock. It was five minutes before eight. In two more hours, I'd know.

"Hey, way to go, Magic," someone said while I was trying to figure out a way to let God know he could give me both things, the spot on the team and a healthy aunt, when Jimmy Oliver patted me on the back. Real hard.

"Thanks, Jimmy," I said, staring at him. He'd done something new to his hair since yesterday. It wasn't just a mess. He'd shaved a part right in the middle. Man, did it look weird. "If I could be one tenth as good on the court as you are on the track, I'd be happy."

Jimmy shrugged. "Don't think that's something to aim for, buddy. I'm trading in my Reeboks for a skateboard. Wait till you see it. It's sick."

"Skateboard?" I repeated. "You're gonna give up track and ride around on a skateboard? Are you kidding me?"

"No joke. I decided I'd like to fly. Anytime you want to join me, I'll be down at Duncan's Hill, working on my board. You should try it. You'd like it."

I shook my head. "I don't think that's me," I told him. "With basketball practice, I'll be real busy. I can't believe you're giving up track. I pictured you in the Olympics. Or at least winning the Boston Marathon someday. No one runs as fast as you, Jimmy."

"I don't think there's a skateboard marathon or a place in the Olympics for skateboarders," Jimmy told me. "But there's plenty of competitions for skateboarders. But try to grasp this, buddy. I'm in it for the fun."

For once, I wished my dad could be there to talk to Jimmy. I had the funniest feeling that I was losing my old friend, but if I could only find the right words, I could hold on to him. But the words just weren't there. "Anyhow," he said, "I gotta run. Nice going, dude." And he was gone. And Peter was still jumping around like crazy.

I grabbed his arm. "We've got thirty seconds to make

it to homeroom or we're gonna spend our first practice in detention,'' I told him, and he was heading up the stairs three at a time, while I lagged behind, barely managing two at a time. It was only after I got in my seat in homeroom that it hit me. I'd made the sixth-grade basketball team. I was too short and too slow to have accomplished such a goal, but it had happened. It was truly a miracle. If only I could learn how to speak in front of Amelia, and Aunt Marcy was okay, my world would be perfect.

I called my dad at five minutes past ten. Ms. Evans excused me from math when I told her why I had to call him. She was a really nice teacher and I felt comfortable talking to her. I hadn't said the words "breast cancer'' to her, but I had told her my aunt was having a biopsy and I had to call my dad to find out the results. I knew the minute I heard my father's voice that the news was bad. "It's malignant, Benjy,'' he told me as soon as he picked up the phone in his office. I also knew it was a big deal for him to be talking to me at five past the hour. My dad meets with his patients for fifty-five minutes and if I ever need to talk to him during the day I call his office at five minutes before the hour, just when his session is up. This morning, he was making a big exception. "But the doctors are hopeful they got it early. They're doing a lumpectomy now and will check her lymph nodes to see if the cancer has spread. We'll know those results tomorrow. We'll talk about it more at dinner, okay?''

I hung up the phone and knew that my life had changed forever. Somehow or other, God had misunderstood my bargain. I'd won, but Aunt Marcy had lost. I wanted to cry, but I didn't. Instead I went back to math and took the quiz Ms. Evans was giving the class. It was a miracle, but I knew I got all the equations right. Nothing in my life seemed normal. I was so upset about my aunt that I couldn't think straight, but I'd aced my math quiz. I couldn't run fast enough or come anywhere near the rim of the basket for a dunk, but I'd made the basketball team. I was about to save the dog of the prettiest girl I'd ever met, but I couldn't speak one word in her presence. What could possibly happen next? Maybe I'd go buy a skateboard and become the skateboard champion of the world. I passed my paper in and shook my head when Ms. Evans asked how my aunt was. If she could figure out what the shake meant, she was way ahead of everybody else in my life.

Five

That night was even more dismal than my day. Uncle Bobby came for dinner, which the twins ended up having to cook because Mom was tied up with Ellen and the greyhounds. About the only thing the twins can cook is Shake 'n Bake chicken, but that night they decided to make something special to cheer up Elliot and Uncle Bobby. Since Elliot's favorite meal is spaghetti and red meat, which Aunt May never cooks for him, and Uncle Bobby loves red sauces, they were planning to prepare something especially for the two of them. They chose some weird kind of pasta with vegetables and a red sauce they called pasta primavera, and a strange veal dish. For someone who knows her way around the kitchen, that was a pretty big deal. For the twins, who share a brain when it comes to cooking, it was out of sight.

When I got home from basketball practice, I was so sore I could barely walk up the front stairs. Coach Murray had apparently realized he'd made a giant error putting me on the team. He'd also decided to make us run sprints around the gym every time we missed a layup. Since I missed more layups than anyone else on the team, I spent my time running around the gym, while the other guys played basketball. It wasn't that Coach Murray was mean, because he wasn't, but he definitely looked sick every time he watched me play. The only one who gave me any encouragement was Will Sheridan, who patted me on the back three times during practice. I wasn't sure that running sprints around the gym was going to turn me into a great player, but I'd made up my mind that I wasn't going to be a wimp and complain about the coach's singling me out for sprints. I was going to do whatever he wanted me to do, and, in the process, surprise him and everyone else on the team by becoming a good player. By the time I walked into my kitchen, however, I was having serious fears that I might not live long enough to be a surprise.

"It's about time you got home," Jenny said. She had flour in her hair and the front of her blue sweatshirt was all splattered with red. "Where were you, anyhow?"

"I had basketball practice," I told her, and the pleasure I got from speaking those words convinced me I had to live at least another week.

"When are those stupid tryouts going to end?" Jillian asked as she pounded some meat with one of Dad's hammers. Man, did that look gross. "I mean, you're so lousy, Benjy. Why are you still going to tryouts?"

"I said 'practice,' " I repeated, snagging a mushroom out of a pan before either of my sisters could slice off my fingers. "I made the team, in case none of your four eyes saw the list on the gym door."

Both my sisters stopped making their messes.

"You're kidding," Jenny finally answered me. "*You* made the team?"

"Sure did," I said. "Too bad your junior high squad can't cheer at my school games, huh?" Man, was I enjoying this. "It sure would be quite a scene to hear a special Morgan cheer for me from you two Morgans, wouldn't it?"

Jillian wiped her hands on her jeans and stared at me. "I just can't believe the coach took you. You stink."

"So does this dinner," I said. I was beginning to get a little nervous with the whole conversation. I knew I stunk and that it was a miracle I'd made the team and that the coach would probably throw me off the team in a day or two. "What the heck are you pounding the life out of over there?"

Jillian drew her attention back to her creation. "It's veal cacciatore, stupid," she informed me. "We decided to try something special for Uncle Bobby. If you could close your mouth and stop bragging for five minutes, you might be able to figure out how to wash the lettuce for the salad."

"Veal cacciatore?" I repeated. "Are you nuts? You know how Mom feels about veal. It's inhumanely slaughtered and the babies are never let out of their stalls. They're never given solid food. They eat the iron off their bars because they're so deprived of nutrition and vitamins. Mom's never served veal in her whole life."

Jenny fixed me a look so filled with hatred I got scared. She was cutting vegetables with a sharp knife and I knew from experience that she has a great aim when provoked. "Mom's not coming home," she informed me through her clenched teeth. "She's visiting

Aunt Marcy right now and then driving to New Hampshire to see Ellen. Daddy loves veal and told us it would be okay for one night since Uncle Bobby needs cheering up."

"And you don't have to eat one mouthful if it's against your religion," Jillian told me. "As a matter of fact, it would make it a lot easier for all of us if you'd eat at a friend's house tonight. That is, if you could find a friend that would be willing to feed your fat face. Hey, maybe . . . " She stopped for a second and smiled real weirdly at Jenny and then turned an evil smile on me. "Maybe you could get Amelia Parker to feed you. At least that would be one way she could see you open your mouth."

Most of the time, I ignore what my sisters say to me. So much of it is so mean, it would make an ordinary person fall apart. But I've been living with them for twelve years, and there isn't anything awful they haven't already said to me. But hearing Jillian talk about Amelia and my locked jaw really knocked me for a loop. If we'd been in a boxing ring, I would say she'd delivered a TKO. I guess it must have showed on my face because Jillian didn't stop, but made sure I didn't get up before the count was finished. "Honestly, Benjy," she continued, "I nearly died when I heard how you acted in your homeroom this morning. You're such a geek. It's embarrassing to be related to you."

"How did you hear?" I asked when I could speak, because I really needed to know. I was certain no one but Peter and Amelia knew about my muteness, and I could not believe either of them would tell the twins about it.

"Jacqueline Buck was delivering a sheet from the

junior high office to your homeroom and she couldn't help noticing the scene you created," Jenny informed me. "Seriously, Benjy, since when have you had such a problem around girls? Maybe the fact that you're such a toilet mouth around your sisters has caused you to have a major problem with your tongue. Too bad, 'cause Jacqueline says Amelia's a beauty. At least Peter can speak around her."

That did it. I could take just so much at one time. I picked up a loaf of heavy Italian bread that was sitting on the counter and hurled it at Jenny's head. She ducked and the loaf landed in the red sauce cooking in a pot on the stove. As the red sauce scattered everywhere, and I mean everywhere, my sisters screamed at me. They would have come after me, but when I'm not on the basketball court, I am fast. And I didn't shout one word back at them as I made my hasty exit.

I was shocked that after lying miserably on my bed, staring at my ceiling for close to an hour, I had any desire for dinner. I was trying to figure out a way I could transfer to another school in another district, or another city, or another state. It was so lousy that our elementary school had to be connected to the twins' junior high. It wasn't bad enough I had to live in the same house as the two of them. I also had to go to their school. Plus, I couldn't get the big orange ball to fall through the hoop or my mouth to open around Amelia Parker. Life just wasn't fair. But when Elliot came into my room to tell me dinner was ready and that my dad was home, I decided to hang on for a little longer and eat maybe one last meal. I knew that if my sisters knew about my silence around Amelia, the entire world knew, and I was the laughingstock of the whole school. That fact, joined with the idea that Peter would probably steal Amelia from me before I could speak one complete sentence to her, convinced me I could never go back to school. But I couldn't hurt Elliot by staying holed up in my room for dinner. For his sake, I had to eat. Plus, the rumblings in my stomach were awfully loud.

"So, how's your mom look?" I asked Elliot as we walked downstairs together. I could tell from looking at the kid that he was a lot more depressed than I was. His mom had cancer. I had just made a fool out of myself. His misery had big-time reasons. By comparison, mine was small potatoes.

"Not bad," he answered. "She's got a big bandage. Right here." He pointed to his chest. "And she can't move much. She's got cancer, you know."

I tousled his hair and sat down on the bottom step. I could hear my sisters and Uncle Bob talking in the kitchen. My dad was on the telephone. Elliot sat down beside me. He was practically on my lap. "I know," I said. "But they got it early. She's going to be fine."

He looked me right in the eye. "You don't think she's going to die, do you?" he asked in a soft voice. I shook my head. "Because in *Snow White* she's just sleeping. She wakes up when the prince kisses her. But in *Lion King* the bad lion kills Simba's father. He doesn't wake up. He's dead forever."

I put my arm around him and lifted him completely onto my lap. "I know all about that," I said. "But your mom is not going to die like Simba's father. She's going to get lots of medicine and get better. I promise you that." I was a little scared making a promise like that to Elliot. After all, what did I know about breast cancer?

41

But I couldn't let him be so frightened. I had to say something to help him feel better.

Elliot looked up at me and sighed. Then he stood up and reached for my hand. "I'm hungry," he told me as we walked into the kitchen. The room was still a terrible mess, but the twins had cleaned up most of the spaghetti sauce from the walls and floor. Elliot pointed to a big pot on top of the stove. "They made us spaghetti," he said, smiling. "I love spaghetti."

I was also surprised that the twins had set six places for dinner. Since Mom wasn't coming home, that meant they expected to feed me. Considering the mess I'd made and my refusal to make the salad, that was surprising. Not nice or anything like that. Just surprising. Uncle Bobby looked real tired, but he smiled as soon as he saw me. "Aunt Marcy left a message for you," he told me, using his Indian accent, which wasn't bad but nowhere as good as Aunt Marcy's, which was so perfect it was scary. "She said she'd love you to get her a Slurpy at the 7-Eleven and bring it to the hospital tomorrow anytime you could manage it."

I laughed and speaking in my own Indian voice, which was better than Uncle Bobby's but inferior to Aunt Marcy's, announced, "My pleasure, of course."

The twins had just finished filling our plates with food that slightly but not strongly resembled veal cacciatore and pasta primavera with a red sauce when my dad walked into the kitchen, shaking his head. "That was Mom," he informed us. "She's on her way to New Hampshire now. Something big's going on with Ellen, but she's not sure exactly what. She'll call us as soon as she gets there."

I glanced at Elliot and saw that he was already trying

42

to pick up his spaghetti with his fork. Luckily, he hadn't understood exactly what my father was talking about. For a psychiatrist, my father could be pretty dense. Elliot was as nutty over the greyhounds as I was. The last thing that kid needed was to be worried about the greyhounds. I wasn't sure exactly why, but I had a definite feeling that Elliot had every right to be worried. Something was wrong in New Hampshire. I knew that just as well as I knew that Aunt Marcy had cancer and I had a social disease whose main symptom was muteness around beautiful girls.

Elliot seemed pretty happy with his spaghetti, but Uncle Bobby, Dad, and I had a tough time getting the veal down. I felt guilty about eating veal, but I figured the poor little things were already dead, so I might as well eat them. Unfortunately, those little calves died in vain. The twins had overcooked the meat so badly it was unchewable. Uncle Bobby and Dad gave it a good shot, but I quit after my first futile attempt to get the meat from my mouth into my throat. A person can chew for just so long before he has to surrender. I had polished off the spaghetti and salad before the phone rang and Mom informed us that the baby calves were not the only animals who were being mistreated big time.

Six

The story was unbelievable. Some insane person or people had come to the farm when Ellen and her farm-hands were at an Adopt-a-Greyhound fund-raiser and viciously attacked all the greyhounds and set fire to the barn. They'd thrown paint all over the dogs and tied them all together. And those were only a few of the terrible things they'd done. "I can't even describe to you what's happened to these dogs," my mother told me. I was the one who answered the phone after dinner and heard the horrible news directly from her. I'd never heard my mom sound that upset. My dad was on the other line, talking to his medical service, and the twins and Elliot and Uncle Bob were finishing their dessert. "I nearly died when I walked in and saw the scene," my mom continued. She was talking real fast. Even though she wasn't crying, she sounded worse than if she were. "Thank God, I had Sheryl with me or I would have fainted on the spot. Ellen had this weird feeling something was going to happen. She's been getting crank calls for two days now. But never in our wildest nightmares could we have imagined this. Those poor dogs, Benjy. Those poor innocent dogs. Two of them are already dead from dehydration and trauma. The other nine are in pretty bad shape, and there's another one that I don't think will make it through the night."

"Do you want us to come up and help?" I asked, desperate to do something to help. "I can have Dad or Uncle Bobby drive us up. We can be there in less than two hours. Okay?"

"No, Benjy," my mom said. She was a little calmer now. Not a lot calmer, but a little bit. "I appreciate your offer, but there are four vets here now, and Ellen and all her farmhands are doing everything they can to save the dogs. I'll call you as soon as I have more information. I've got to run now. You tell Dad what's happening but don't tell Elliot yet. Somehow, I'll get home tomorrow to see Aunt Marcy. It kills me to tell you such terrible news like this, Benjy, but it's going to be all over the newspapers and television tomorrow. Hopefully, we can keep it away from Elliot until I can tell him about it myself. But I wanted you of all people to hear it from me."

"Sure, Mom," I said, feeling sicker by the second. "I understand."

"Benjy," she began, and then she stopped. "Oh, I've got to go. Someone is calling me. Sorry. Bye, Benjy."

And she was gone. It took a big effort for me to hang up the phone and rejoin my family in the kitchen. My dad was still on the other phone, but everyone else was sitting around the table enjoying dessert. Uncle Bobby and Elliot had picked up ice cream from Friendly's on their way home from the hospital, and, luckily, there was no way the twins could destroy that part of the meal. Elliot had a huge smile on his face as Jillian told him a story about a cat who always wore a purple raincoat. One thing Jillian was good at was making up stories. Once, about two years ago, when I'd been sick with pneumonia and she must have thought I was on my way out, she'd spent hours telling me her wild stories. As soon as she found out I was going to survive, she stopped telling me anything but insults. Still, it had been terrific while it lasted.

"So what's going on with Mom?" Jenny asked as I sat down and tried to eat my melting ice cream. Like the veal, the ice cream wouldn't get down my throat. "Is there really something wrong at Ellen's? I know she's been acting weird and nervous and Mom was worried about her and the greyhounds."

I shrugged my shoulders. "No big deal," I lied, and Jenny refilled her dish with chocolate chip ice cream.

Elliot's eyes were glued to Jillian's face, but Uncle Bobby was looking at me strangely. As soon as I got up to rinse out my dish, he followed me to the sink. "Need some help with your math homework?" he asked me.

"Sure," I answered and led the way to my room. "It's real bad, Uncle Bobby," I told him as soon as we hit my room. I could feel the tears filling up my eyes, but I was determined not to cry. "Some maniac broke into Ellen's barn and tried to kill all the greyhounds. A few are dead and some more might die. My mom sounds real bad. Why would anyone do something like that?"

Uncle Bobby sat down on my bed and shook his head. "God only knows," he said. "There are a lot of

crazies out there. Your dad can testify to that. Maybe
we should head up there after we get Elliot to bed and
see if we can help.''

"I suggested that," I told him, "but Mom didn't
think that was a good idea.''

"Well, she knows best," he said. "I guess all we
can do is just wait and hope that the rest of the dogs
will be all right. I know how much you love the greyhounds, Benjy. This must be real rough for you.''

"Oh, I'm okay," I said and tried to act like it was
true. "But what about you? You've already got so much
to worry about. I mean, with Aunt Marcy and
everything.''

"I might be the stupidest man on the face of the
earth," he said, "but I believe she's going to be fine.
I'm just grateful that we found the cancer this early. I'm
convinced the news we'll get about her lymph glands
tomorrow will be good. Besides, you know your Aunt
Marcy. She has too much to do with keeping all us
Simpsons in shape to check out early.'' He smiled.
"You know how all the Simpsons always land on their
feet? God, remember that show with their dog which
was on its way out, but it pulled through?'' I nodded.
That was one of my all-time favorite *Simpsons*. "Well,
I don't mean to make a joke out of Marcy's illness, but
I know she would. That dog made it and she definitely
will. Am I right or am I right?''

I couldn't help laughing at Uncle Bobby's comparison. He was right. Aunt Marcy would have loved it. I
felt so good by the time Uncle Bobby left my room that
I could have gone downstairs and swallowed one small
piece of veal cacciatore. But luckily I didn't have to do
that. All I had to do was try and put the greyhounds

47

out of my mind for a few minutes and talk to Elliot before he fell asleep. Then, I could tell my father and the twins what my mother had told me.

"Are you kids all right with this?" my father kept asking the three of us an hour later after I finished my story about the greyhounds.

The twins had dissolved into tears and I was having a hard time acting cool, but we all nodded at our father. The last thing any of us wanted was a speech from him about the need to express our feelings and not hold anything bottled inside. But, unfortunately, our nods didn't do the trick. "Just because there are some sick people in this world," he told us, in case we didn't already know, "we can't let that convince us the whole world is sick. Still, this is a terrible shock. I want you all to talk about it with me now so it doesn't eat you up inside."

"I don't want to talk abut it," Jenny said, and to prove her point she got up and left the room.

"Me, neither," Jillian said and followed her twin out of the family room.

"I'm bushed," I told my father, but he wasn't going to lose his chance to unbottle one of his kids.

"I know you are," he said, "but you're the one who heard the story directly from Mom. How did that make you feel, Benjy."

"Terrible," I answered.

"Terrible?" he repeated. "What exactly does terrible mean here?"

"It means it made me sick, Dad. But now I'm tired. And I really want to go to bed."

"Are you angry at your mom?" he asked me, and I sighed.

"No," I answered. "Why would I be angry at Mom? I'm just tired."

"I don't want you to feel it's wrong to be angry with your mother," he informed me. "Because it isn't. It's okay. But it's not okay to deny the anger. Parents are not perfect and sometimes we do things that bring unhappiness to our children. If your mother were a teacher or waitress, she might not have come into contact with this ugliness. Don't you wish she hadn't?"

"I guess so," I said. "But I love the greyhounds as much as she does. But, really, Dad, I'm so tired I feel sick."

"I understand," he told me. "You need time to be alone and put everything into perspective for yourself. You just have to be sure to remember that everyone is to blame here. And it's okay to blame anyone you want and to be angry."

I felt bad leaving my dad alone. I knew he meant well and that it wouldn't have been such a terrible thing to have let him fix up my mind a little, but I wasn't in the mood for a brain shampoo. I'd had enough for one day. As a matter of fact, I'd had enough for a thousand days. Without another word to anyone or even a quick glance at my math homework, I crawled under my covers and immediately fell asleep. And dreamed about greyhounds. Sad-eyed greyhounds that were sinking into a huge quivering pile of quicksand. I tried everything I could, but I couldn't save them. All I could do was watch as one by one the sand swallowed them up, covering their big black eyes until there was nothing left of each beautiful dog.

As if that dream wasn't enough, I had a second dream. This one had quicksand in it, only this time, it was a herd of white lhasa apsos that were being swallowed up and the last one to go was named Boo Boo. ''Save him, Benjy!'' a sweet voice kept pleading with me, but I had tape around my entire body, as well as my mouth, and I couldn't move. So Boo Boo drowned in the quicksand, and so did I.

Seven

Elliot was restless all night. Between his tossing, turning, and crying out in his sleep and my dog nightmares, I got the worst night of sleep ever. Elliot was very quiet at breakfast and I knew he missed his mother a lot. Uncle Bobby was as good as he could be with him and so were the twins, but that morning I was the only one he wanted to be with. "I wish my mother was coming home today," he told me. He was sitting on the bathtub watching me brush my teeth after breakfast. I nodded sympathetically. When I finished brushing, he picked up his toothbrush and brushed his teeth very slowly and carefully. Finally, he put down his toothbrush and was cleaning the toothpaste out of the sink with toilet paper. "I like it here, but I miss my own house," he informed me once the sink was as clean as his teeth.

"You can sleep there tonight if you want," I reminded him. "Your dad said he'll do whatever you want."

"I know," he agreed. "But I don't want to sleep there without my mother. It's too lonely. Here, it's not as lonely. But, still, I miss my mother."

"I know what you mean," I said as I helped him replace a Band-Aid on his thumb. There didn't seem to be any cut there, but he liked the Flintstones Band-Aids and wanted a Bam Bam picture on the front of his thumb. "I kind of miss my mom, too, and I'm a lot older than you."

Elliot stared at me real hard for a minute. "I miss Auntie Carol, too," he said. "When is she coming home from New Hampshire?"

We'd all been real careful not to let Elliot know what was going on at Ellen's farm. None of us needed my father to explain how tough this would all be for Elliot to digest. He was crazy about the greyhounds and always played with them when he came to the shelter. He'd even come up to Ellen's farm with us a couple of times. With all he was going through with his mother's illness, the last thing he needed was to be upset about the nightmare in New Hampshire. "Probably tonight," I said. "Tomorrow night, at the latest."

"That's good," he said, and then turned his concentration back to Bam Bam's face. " 'Cause that means we'll both have our moms back where they belong."

Uncle Bobby had just left to drive Elliot to kindergarten when my mom called again. First, she spoke to each twin. Then, she spoke to me. A third greyhound had died during the night. It was a black-and-white dog, named Lucky, my ultimate favorite greyhound. Lucky had come to the shelter from a lab at Morton University, a veterinary school in Boston. My mother hated Dr. Lewis, a track veterinarian who also ran this lab, more than she hated anyone else in the world. I knew that labs did terrible things to dogs and cats. Some of the experiments were supposed to be to test drugs that could save the lives of humans and were needed to help find cures for dreaded diseases. Some labs did these experiments mercifully and with little if any pain to the poor animals. But, according to my mom, many experiments were done for other reasons, to raise money for labs and to show results that had already been proven.

Greyhounds are favorite subjects for most experiments. They're very passive and gentle, used to living in small crates and being muzzled. They practically never bite anyone, not even people who are torturing them in labs. Since there are several dog-racing tracks surrounding Boston, there is always a steady stream of greyhounds available for experimentation. Dr. Lewis is big on what he calls "long-term survival projects," where he makes the greyhounds participate in controversial bone-replacement experiments. My mother is constantly hounding our congressmen about this lab. She thinks nothing about marching right into the lab and checking on Dr. Lewis's experiments herself. She's also set up letter writing campaigns against the lab and Dr. Lewis and written numerous newspaper articles about animal experiments.

Lucky had been locked up in Dr. Lewis's lab for three months before my mother heard about him. It was unbelievable what cruel things had been done to that dog, but he had survived. My mother has several spies from that lab and when it became evident that Lucky was going to die, they alerted her. The next day, my mother appeared at the lab before it opened, released Lucky from his cage, and brought him to the shelter.

Dr. Lewis knew what had happened, but he also knew my mother wouldn't hesitate to call every major newspaper in Boston to take pictures of poor Lucky at her shelter. Unfortunately, my mother can't save all the dogs Dr. Lewis kills and tortures, but she sure does have a strong record of heroic rescues. I don't think of my mother as a violent person, but I know she'd do anything to put Dr. Lewis to sleep.

The minute I saw Lucky, I fell in love with him. I have to admit I'm real partial to greyhounds, but that's because of the large number of them that have come to the shelter. I don't understand how anybody could spend an hour with a greyhound and not come away loving the animal. The fact that they're so abused by the track and labs makes me love them even more.

Lucky lived at our house for a couple of weeks while my mother and her favorite vet, Dr. Parisi, nursed him back to health. I kept him in my room at night and he slept on a blanket at the end of my bed. Only somehow or other every night after I'd fallen asleep, Lucky would end up with his head on my pillow. It was the most amazing thing. Every morning I would wake up and the first thing I would see was Lucky's two big brown eyes staring at me. He was so weak he could barely move, but still he scooted up to my pillow and laid his head on it every night. I had to carry him up and down the stairs for two weeks. Most greyhounds have trouble with stairs since they've been trained to run in a straight line, but Lucky didn't have the strength to walk anywhere, never mind trot up the stairs. He weighed practically nothing, but still he would rest his head on my shoulder when I carried him up and down the stairs. Man, did that get to me.

He was so human, it was scary. He'd wait by the window until I came home from school, which is something lots of dogs do while waiting for their owners to return, but Lucky had very little energy and to keep his head against that window cost him a lot of it. But there was nothing my mother could do to make him lie down and wait for me. As soon as I came home, he lay down and slept.

It was great to watch him grow stronger every day, and by the time he left us to go to Ellen's farm, he had gained back all his weight and was able to walk long distances. My mom and Ellen were worried about how he would do without me around, but Lucky managed just fine. He'd only been at Ellen's six months before he died. The worst part of the whole thing was that Ellen was putting the finishing touches on an adoption for Lucky with a family with a lot of property and three little kids. Lucky would have loved that family. But some insane person had prevented him from ever living with them.

When I hung up the phone from my mom, I went upstairs to wash my face. There was no way I could stop the tears. To think of all that dog had survived and how he had died just drove me out of my mind. Jillian banged on the bathroom door while I was washing my face and crying. "Enough already, Benjy!" she shouted through the door. "I've got to get in there now!"

I turned off the faucet and opened the door for her. "Man, do you look weirder than normal," she informed me as I slid past her.

"Wait till you see what's waiting for you in the bathroom mirror," I told her, shaking my head in disgust as I stared at her nose. "I just hope you can handle it 'cause it's not a pretty scene. Especially that big red thing sitting on top of your nose like it owns the world. Hey, Rudolph. Where did you park your sleigh?" I felt better when she slammed the door real hard. Not great, but a tiny bit better.

Eight

Amelia Parker wasn't at my desk in homeroom that morning, but Wendy Brown was. "I heard about the greyhounds," she told me, shaking her head from side to side. "What a horrible thing. You must be a wreck."

Wendy looked real upset. She'd spent a lot of time with Lucky when he was at my house and at the shelter. She'd even had her mom drive her up to New Hampshire a couple of times to visit him. But she floored me with her news. I didn't mean to be so fierce, but I grabbed her arm and held it real tightly. "How did you hear about them?" I practically shouted at her. All I could think about was Elliot finding out about the greyhound tragedy from someone other than me. "Don't tell me it was on the news already."

"I saw it on the early news this morning," she said, removing my hand from her arm. "Geez, Benjy, I'm sorry. I figured you saw it on the news. Your mom was there, talking to the reporter. She looked awful."

I let my hand fall to my side. "Wow," I said. "I forgot my mom said it was going to be on the news. I haven't even told Elliot."

"You better tell him soon," Wendy said. " 'Cause it's bound to be in the newspapers this afternoon. Maybe you can get Amelia to give you an advance copy of the afternoon edition."

The way she said it was real funny. I'd never heard her sound that way before. Kind of sarcastic and mean. I ignored her tone. I had news to give her which I knew would hurt her deeply. "Lucky died last night," I told her quickly. I figured the sooner I got those words out, the better. "My mom told me before I left for school."

Wendy leaned against my desk and closed her eyes. I could see the tears welling up in the corners of her eyes. The last thing I wanted was to have her get hysterical right here in homeroom. It was amazing. My desk at homeroom was becoming an emotional battlefield. One day Amelia Parker turns me into a dumb mute. The next day, I'm shoving Wendy Brown and making her dissolve into tears in the same spot. Peter Chandler walked into homeroom at that exact moment, and once again came to my rescue.

"Hey, what's up, you two?" he asked casually. Then he took a long look at Wendy. "You sick or something, Wendy?" he asked. "What's the matter with both of you, anyhow?" Before I could answer, he answered his own question. "Oh, I bet you're upset about the greyhounds, huh? Man, that was awful. Is there anything I can do to help, Benjy?"

"How'd you hear?" I asked while Wendy rummaged through her pocketbook for some tissue.

"The twins told me," he said. "I just ran into them

in the hall. They were bringing some cheerleader stuff to our office. They looked pretty upset, too. Not as bad as you, Wendy, 'cause your eye stuff is running all over your face, and Jillian and Jenny would never have anything running down their faces. I swear if old Benjy croaked, they still wouldn't have black stuff running down their faces. Maybe they'd cry, but there'd be no running black stuff like with old Wendy.''

''Fat chance of that ever happening,'' I said, glad to see that Wendy was managing a small smile. ''If I ever croaked, the only thing you'd see on the their faces would be two identical huge smiles.''

Suddenly someone else had joined us. I knew by the feeling in my throat, the sensation that my voice had taken another hike, that it could only be Amelia Parker. ''I saw that thing about the greyhounds on the news, Benjy,'' she reported, standing next to Wendy. It was funny but neither one of the girls seemed to notice the other one. ''I heard what your mother had to say about it. She's incredible. I just hope she won't be too busy to help me with Boo Boo on Saturday.''

There is a very slight chance that I might have opened my mouth and answered Amelia. A very slight chance. But I would never know that because before I could get out even a grunt, Wendy was noticing Amelia but good. ''Gee, I sure hope Boo Boo doesn't get inconvenienced by all this greyhound mess,'' she said, her hands on her hips, staring right into Amelia's great big black eyes. '' 'Cause that would be just terrible, wouldn't it?''

''I didn't mean it like that,'' Amelia said. She looked real small standing next to Wendy but, man, did she look pretty. ''It's just that Boo Boo is my dog and he might be put to sleep on Saturday if Benjy's mom doesn't take him into her shelter. That's all I meant."

"Well, for your information," Wendy continued, "Benjy's and my favorite greyhound died in that mess. I'm sure your Boo Boo is a great dog, but we're both in a little bit of mourning now for one incredible dog who suffered a lot in his life and wasn't put to sleep gently. Lucky suffered a terrible death. And he never bit a single human being. Not even one who was torturing him." Before Amelia could say a word, Wendy was gone. I've known Wendy for a long time, but I've never seen her move that quickly. Not even last summer when we were walking down by an abandoned warehouse and a huge man came out of the house and aimed a slingshot at us.

"Wendy loved Lucky," Peter announced, since it was obvious I was back to my mute state and Amelia was ready to cry. "I'm sure she didn't mean to insult you or Boo Boo. She just really loved that greyhound."

"Sure," Amelia said. "I understand. I'll see you at the shelter tomorrow morning, okay?"

"Sure," I said as she walked out of the room, proud that I'd been able to speak after all, but wondering if my mother would even be there tomorrow. It seemed pretty unlikely with all that was going on in New Hampshire that she'd be back at the shelter on Saturday morning, but there was nothing I could do about that now.

My homeroom teacher let me call my father's office. I left a message for him to call Elliot's school so someone there would know what had happened to the greyhounds. I just didn't want Elliot to hear about it from another little kid. I knew my dad would do what had to be done to protect Elliot. Nothing much happened during the rest of my school day, except that I did lousy on my math quiz and Wendy wouldn't speak to me at lunch. But basketball practice was another horror. No matter what I did, Mr. Murray and Will Sheridan were on my case, yelling at me, criticizing me, making me feel like a total idiot. A few minutes before the practice was about to end, I was certain Mr. Murray was going to throw me off the team. Just my luck, the twins appeared in the gym with their cheerleading squad, ready to begin their practice at that exact moment.

"Hi, Benjy," Jillian said, her voice real sleepy and slow. "How's it going, kid?"

I knew from the look on her face that she had seen and heard everything the coach had just screamed at me. I tried to dribble the ball away from my sisters, but they were too quick for me. "Rough day, Benjy?" Jenny practically shouted across the court.

I was considering hurling the basketball at their heads. With my lousy aim, I would probably have missed both of them and knocked out Will Sheridan, who had stopped insulting me and was looking at the two blond heads I wanted to shatter. Since the coach wasn't looking at me, I made two layups and was executing another brilliant move around Peter when I glanced back at Will. He couldn't get his eyes off the two identical girls who were standing at the edge of the court, staring at me, waiting hopefully for me to fall flat on my face. When their practice mercifully began, they abandoned their spots and joined the rest of their squad. Suddenly, Will was beside me, only this time he wasn't insulting me.

"Nice play, Morgan," he told me. "I guess you play better when you have an audience, huh?"

I nodded. "I'm working on my footwork like you and the coach said," I told him. "You know, trying to move on the balls of my feet instead of . . ."

"You continue to do that," he interrupted me, and came a little bit closer. "Now, tell me something, Benjy. Those sisters of yours, have they ever mentioned my name around your house?"

I'm not a totally stupid person. I might get mute around beautiful girls, but I understood what was happening here. Will liked my sisters. He'd obviously used his clout to get Coach Murray to put me on the team in the first place. Part of me wanted to hand in my basketball jersey and answer, "Find your own dates, Will." But the other part was in charge here. "Yeah, they do now," I lied. "A lot. But that's 'cause they're so interested in everything I do. We're unbelievably close, the three of us. We stick up for one another. Always." Since I'd already started a good lie, I figured I might as well finish it up in grand style. "Yup, the three of us. We're one solid team. Jenny, Jillian and Benjy Morgan. One for all and all for one." Peter had come over to where I was standing at the end of my speech and I could see the expression on his face. I threw the ball at him before he could throw up.

"Be sure and write your phone numbers on the roster on my desk before you leave today," Will told us at the end of our practice. "The coach or I might have to call you guys to change a practice or schedule a scrimmage. I'll just call one or two of you and have you call the others." I understood who one of those two would be. And I also understood there was no way I could convince my sisters to go out with him so I could stay on the team. Things were looking pretty tough for the kid, but I wasn't about to worry about all that now. I'd survived being ejected from the team today. I was a lot luckier than poor Lucky.

Nine

Before I went home that afternoon, I stopped at the hospital to see Aunt Marcy. I knew she was coming home the next morning, but I couldn't wait that long to see her. When I walked into her room, she was all alone, sitting in a chair, staring at a tray filled with hospital food. I saw her before she saw me. She looked unbelievably sad. But the minute she saw me, her face brightened and she gave me a warm smile. "Ah, so there you are, Apu," she said in her best Simpson accent, characterizing the Indian owner of the 7-Eleven just perfectly. "It is about time you have arrived. I have been waiting for my cinnamon Slurpy for a very long while."

I handed her the strawberry Slurpy from the 7-Eleven near the hospital, bowing respectfully from my waist. I wished I could have found her a cinnamon Slurpy, but that exists only on *The Simpsons*. "It is my pleasure to serve you, my dear woman," I said, my accent not as strong as hers, but a pretty decent attempt. "You know, do you not, that I had another robbery at my store." She looked at me in mock horror as I lifted my shirt and pointed to my chest. "Yes, here is my forty-fifth bullet wound. But, do not worry. I am fine. I shall recover and will work another forty-eight-hour shift tonight. It is never too much for me to labor at my 7-Eleven."

She took a few sips of the Slurpy and smiled at me. "A most delicious treat," she said, and then she put down both the Slurpy and the accent. "But tell me, Benjy. Have you seen Elliot today? Uncle Bob told me he wasn't at his after-school program. He was sure your father or you or the twins must have picked him up instead, but I'm not sure exactly where he is. Have you seen him?"

Man, did my insides flop. It was like a nightmare come true. Ever since Wendy had mentioned the newscast to me in homeroom, I'd had this horrible image of Elliot taking off and my being unable to find him. I struggled to make my face look normal, but I must have done a terrible job because Aunt Marcy looked like I felt: terrified.

"You don't know where he is, do you?" she asked me.

"No," I admitted, "but I haven't been home since seven-thirty this morning. I'd bet anything Dad or the twins took him somewhere." I was lying through my teeth about the twins. I'd seen them at their cheerleading practice and there was no Elliot near either one of them.

"Well, do me a favor and see if you can locate your father or the twins and find out what's going on," Aunt

Marcy said. "No one's answered at your house or mine all afternoon."

I used the phone by her bed to call my house, but there was still no answer. I called my father's office, but got his secretary. He'd left his office an hour earlier. She promised to page him and have him call my aunt in the hospital as soon as she could find him. I called three of the twins' friends, but they weren't at their homes. "The twins were still in the middle of their practice when I left the gym," I told my aunt, but she just shook her head and looked more worried by the second.

"What the heck is going on here?" she asked me. "I haven't heard a word from Elliot since he called me this morning before he left for nursery school. He calls at least four times a day. Bob sounded pretty upset. Now, I'm really beginning to panic."

So was I. Uncle Bobby should have called her and let her know exactly what was going on. I tried to change the subject and told Aunt Marcy about my problems with Will Sheridan, but I could see that she wasn't concentrating on what I was saying. "Do me a favor and go home and see what's happening there," she urged me. "And call me as soon as you get there. If I don't hear from Elliot in a half hour, I'm out of this stupid hospital. The last thing I'm going to do is sit here if no one knows where Elliot is."

"I don't blame you," I said and kissed her quickly on the cheek before I left. I knew in my heart that she had every reason to be panicked. Something had happened to Elliot.

When I got home, my worst fears were confirmed. My father and Uncle Bobby walked in two minutes after

66

me, and the looks on their faces told the story. Elliot was nowhere to be found. "He's been missing for an hour," Uncle Bobby told me. "I picked him up from school and stopped at our house to get a few things for Aunt Marcy to wear home tomorrow. As soon as we got to the house, I told him about the greyhounds as gently as I could, but I guess I did a lousy job. He just stared at me and started crying. Then the phone rang and I should never have answered it, but I did. It was one of the guys from my office with an important message for me. I wrote it down quickly and hung up, and when I looked around the kitchen, Elliot was gone. I searched the whole house, screaming his name in every room, but I couldn't find him. I called your father and the police. It's been wild, but I don't know where he took off to. Do you have any idea where he might have gone?"

"None," I said. "Maybe he's trying to get to the hospital to see his mother."

"I can't believe he'd do that," Uncle Bobby said. "I told him we were going there as soon as I got her clothes together."

"Maybe he was looking for you, Benjy," my father suggested. "You know how crazy he is about you. Plus, he knows how important the greyhounds are to you, too."

"He knew I had basketball practice," I said. "Did you drive over to the gym or check the streets leading from our house to his?"

"We just did that," my father said. "No sign of him. It's crazy. How far could a five-year-old go in such a short time? It just doesn't make any sense."

"Aunt Marcy knows something's up," I told them.

67

"I just came from visiting her. I promised I'd call her as soon as I got home or else she's leaving the hospital."

"I'd better get right over there," Uncle Bobby said, "and try to convince her I know where Elliot is."

"She'll never believe you," my father said. "You're going to have to tell her the truth and if she wants to leave the hospital, she should. She has a right to know what's going on with Elliot. She's physically strong enough to handle it all now. Don't lie to her."

"Okay," Uncle Bobby said. "Don't forget. I'm on beeper. Call me if you hear anything. I'll call and let you know if Marcy wants out of there."

"I'll be on beeper, too," my father said. "I'm going to wait here for the police. Any place you can think of looking, Benjy?"

My mind was a blank, but suddenly I thought of Jimmy Oliver. I have no idea why he came into my mind. I'd seen him as I was leaving the gym. He was skateboarding outside in the parking lot. He'd been moving like lightning. All I could think of was Jimmy scouring the whole town, looking for Elliot on his vicious skateboard. "I'll make a few calls," I said, and ran upstairs to my room to call Jimmy.

He answered on the first ring. "Hey, man," he greeted me. "What's up? I just saw your mom on TV. Amazing what happened to those greyhounds."

"My little cousin Elliot is missing," I told him. "He's upset about the greyhounds and his mother's cancer. Can you help me look for him?"

"Hey, wow," Jimmy said. "I'll be right over. You can hitch a ride on my big skateboard. Elliot's the neatest little guy around. We'll find him."

I felt the first flutter of hope since I'd walked into

68

Aunt Marcy's hospital room. Before I ran outside to meet Jimmy, I called Peter. He promised to check out the local playgrounds and scour the area near Elliot's house. He said he'd call Wendy, too, because she does a lot of baby-sitting and knows little kids like Elliot real well. Jimmy was waiting the minute I walked out my back door. I couldn't believe how quickly he'd gotten to my house from his. I don't think a car could have made it that fast. "Hop on," he ordered me, and I took a deep breath and did as he said. I've ridden a skateboard many times before, but I've never been on one with another person. Especially someone who moves as fast as Jimmy. "Try and keep your feet up on the board and let me do the work," he ordered me.

It wasn't easy but I followed his instructions, and before I knew it we were at the school playground. For the next two hours, Jimmy took us all over town, to every playground and store and street within a five-mile radius of Elliot's house. It was unbelievably difficult looking for a little guy like Elliot. There were so many buildings he could have gone into or yards he could be hiding in. It was like looking for a needle in a haystack.

When it started to get dark, we headed back to my house for flashlights. The twins were in the kitchen, making sandwiches. "Hi," Jillian said to me. She looked exhausted, too tired to insult me in her usual manner. "No luck, huh?" Then she noticed Jimmy standing behind me. "Oh, hi, Jimmy," she said to him. "I heard you were helping look for Elliot. That's cool. Want a turkey sandwich?"

Jimmy suddenly looked real nervous. Out there on the streets, he was a demon, steering that skateboard in and out of streets like a fearless navigator. But now, looking at my sister, he was all tongue-tied. It was amazing what effect those twins had on normal guys. Before Jimmy could answer, Jenny was handing him a sandwich on a paper plate. "I guess you guys had no luck," she said.

"We looked everywhere," I said as I took the sandwich Jillian gave me. It was on white bread, which my mother never allows us to eat. I love the soft fluffy feel of that bread. It tastes so much better than the dark, heavy, healthy bread my mom always serves. That night, however, I had no appetite. Just thinking of Elliot out there in the dark alone made me want to throw up. "It's really getting scary."

"I'm going to go back out," Jimmy said. I couldn't help noticing how weird he looked. His hair was back to being spiked. Flying around on the skateboard had made it wilder than usual, and I noticed for the first time that he'd dyed a little bit of one side red. He was wearing a black leather jacket with a skull and bones on the back, and he even had a dangling silver earring in his right ear. If I hadn't known what a great kid he'd been those past two hours, I might have been more than a little bit afraid of him. "I can get around faster if I do it solo, buddy," he told me as he shoved his sandwich into his jacket pocket and took off without another word.

The rest of the evening was a nightmare. The only good part was that my mom got home a few minutes after Jimmy left, but did she look terrible. A lot worse than Aunt Marcy had looked in the hospital. "I just came from Aunt Marcy's house," she told us after she hugged each one of us so tightly, even Jenny cried out. And Jenny's tough like nails. "She's glued to the window with the portable phone in her hand. I'm worried sick about her. She's barely recovered from her surgery and look what she's going through now. The police keep saying they're not worried, that it's just a case of a little boy who is upset and took off to be by himself for a few hours. They say he'll come home any second. But what do they know? They've never said two words to Elliot. He's no ordinary five-year-old. He'd never do something like this to his mother.''

"Oh, Mommy, where is he?" Jillian started to cry and, of course, two seconds later, Jenny was sobbing, too. The truth was I felt like crying, too, but I bit the insides of my cheeks so I wouldn't. Every time I looked outside and saw how dark and cold it was out there, I couldn't stand it. Where was Elliot? Was he cold and scared? Was he lost? Had someone taken him away from us? I couldn't bear to think of all the horrible things that might have happened to him. I knew my father, Uncle Bobby, Jimmy and the police were still out there looking for him, but with every passing minute, I got more panicked about my little cousin.

Peter called me around nine o'clock that night. "I know there's no news or you would have called me," he said.

"There isn't," I told him. "And I'm not supposed to use the phone for too long in case Elliot's trying to call us."

"Sure," Peter agreed. "But I just wanted you to know that Wendy is still out there looking for Elliot."

"She is?" I asked. "By herself?"

"No, she's got her mom out there with her. They're driving around aimlessly, I guess. She keeps calling me

71

on her mom's car phone to ask if anything's happened. Don't forget and call me the second you hear anything."

"I won't," I promised and after I hung up I pictured Wendy in her mom's big red Jeep, driving all over town, looking for Elliot. Sometimes that girl acted so weird. Like she had around Amelia. But tonight, she was my old friend that I'd hung around with in elementary school. Girls sure were impossible to figure out. Just when I figured I had enough to keep my brain on overload for the rest of my life, the phone rang again. It was for me again. "A girl!" Jillian shouted upstairs to me. "And make it quick, lover boy. You've been tying up the line all night." It was good to know my sisters were acting at least a little bit normal despite our family's nightmare.

And what a girl it was. "Hi, Benjy," the female voice began. "It's Amelia Parker. I hope I'm not bothering you."

"No," I answered, a big deal for me.

"Oh, that's good because I just wanted to remind you about tomorrow morning. You see, Boo Boo had a bad night tonight. My mother had a couple of her friends over for some kind of a stupid meeting and one of her friends sat on the couch. That couch is very special to Boo Boo. It's like his bed. I mean, he has his own bed, but the couch is like part of his bed because it's right near where we keep his bed.

"Anyhow, one of my mother's friends, Karen is her name, sat down on the couch and was talking real loudly. Boo Boo was in his bed, but Karen's voice must have disturbed him, because the next thing you know, Boo Boo is up on the couch, and he sort of leaned over as if he might bite her arm. He didn't bite her arm and he probably wouldn't have, but Karen screamed so loud she scared poor Boo Boo half out of his mind, and he grabbed on to her sleeve.

"You should have seen it, Benjy. It was such a terrible scene. My mother screamed at Boo Boo and tried to pull him off Karen's sleeve, but she just got him more upset and he sort of growled at her. Somehow I was able to get poor Boo Boo out of there without any more trouble, but the damage was done. My mother and her friend were wrecks. My mother said that's it. She said my father was absolutely right about Boo Boo. Boo Boo's out of here. I told her about the shelter and she said I can keep Boo Boo until tomorrow and that's that. So, I just have to be sure I can bring Boo Boo over there tomorrow. I know you said it was okay in school today, but you were kind of quiet and I heard about the greyhound thing. But I just wanted to remind you that Boo Boo and I will be at the shelter by nine tomorrow morning. So, is that okay?"

"My cousin's missing," I said. I know that sounds like a ridiculous thing to say to a girl who's just finished this huge, long story about her pathetic dog, but when it comes to Amelia, it's a miracle I can say anything at all. So that might not be all that ridiculous.

"Huh?" she asked.

"He's five," I told her.

"Oh," she answered. "Well, I'm sure you'll find him and, besides, this will only take a few minutes at the shelter. Right?"

"Get off the phone!" I could hear Jillian's shrill voice from outside my door. She was right. I'd been on the phone too long.

"Yeah," I answered Amelia, and then I hung up. I

could picture Amelia's pretty face in front of me. There was no doubt she was the best-looking girl in our whole class, but she sure wasn't the nicest.

The phone rang one minute later, and I figured it was Amelia again. This time I would try to explain to her how worried we all were about Elliot. But it wasn't Amelia. It was Jimmy. He'd found Elliot.

Ten

Elliot was filthy and cold and shaking all over, but he was safe and alive and unbroken. And I've never been so happy to see anyone in my whole life as I was to see Jimmy when he came riding up to Seaside Park with Elliot on the back of his skateboard. "He only wants to see you," Jimmy told me when he called with the news that he'd found Elliot. "He's okay, but he's in pretty bad shape, if you know what I mean."

"I know what you mean," I said, "but I have to tell my parents and aunt and uncle that he's okay. They're out of their minds with worry. Okay?"

"Sure," Jimmy said. "But you're the first one he wants to see. Just tell them that, okay?"

"Sure," I agreed, and ran downstairs to spread the word. My father and the twins were the only ones in our house. Mom was at Aunt Marcy's and Uncle Bobby's.

I couldn't believe how terrific my father was about Elliot's request to see only me. "It's understandable that he's not acting normally," my father said. "Something terrible drove him to run away and we need to treat him very carefully now. I'll tell everybody the good news and convince them all you're doing the right thing. Just go to him and listen to him. Don't preach to him. Let him know you love him and we love him and no one is angry with him for what he did. We're all here when he's ready to see us. Remember, Benjy, he's just a five-year-old little guy. Sometimes, we forget that when we're dealing with him, but he is only five. Hurry and get to that park now."

Jillian handed me a bag filled with brownies as I raced out the door. I knew they were for Elliot, not me, but she didn't scream those words to me. She just handed me the bag and said nothing. It was weird. But everything was weird lately.

Elliot was sitting on a park bench next to Jimmy, who had his arm around him. Man, did Elliot look small. As soon as he saw me, he began to cry. "I didn't mean to be bad," he told me after I sat down beside him and lifted him onto my lap. "I'm sorry, Benjy."

"I understand," I told him when he stopped crying. "I'm just so glad Jimmy found you. We were all looking everywhere. I even came to this park a couple of times tonight and didn't see you here."

"That's 'cause your cousin is an incredible tree climber," Jimmy explained. "I swear, this kid is three parts monkey and one part human. I would never have found him either if he hadn't dropped a walnut onto my head." He rubbed his head and groaned. "Actually, I think it might have been a coconut."

Elliot smiled through his tears. "It wasn't a walnut," he corrected Jimmy. "It was an acorn."

"Sounds like you wanted someone to find you," I said.

"I was awful hungry," Elliot admitted. "I don't think I could have lasted much longer. And I heard some growling. Jimmy said it could have been a bear."

"A bear!" I repeated in mock horror. "You've seen bears around here, Jimmy?"

"Not exactly," Jimmy said. "But I've heard about them. It was just lucky I was here at that time. But let me tell you, if I ever need a good tree climber, I know where to go. I remember when you were five, Benjy. You couldn't climb onto a chair. Are you sure this little runt isn't related to Tarzan?"

Jimmy ruffled Elliot's hair which was already pretty messy. Man, did Elliot look filthy. He had dirt all over his face and leaves stuck in his hair. "Thanks for finding me," he said to Jimmy.

"No problem," Jimmy answered him. "But I better get going now. I got some science homework to do."

I couldn't help but smile at that one. Jimmy hadn't opened his science book yet. Still, I was glad he was going. I knew Elliot had a story to tell me and the sooner I got that story out of him, the sooner I could get him home where he belonged.

"See you, Jimmy," Elliot said as Jimmy got on his skateboard and headed out of the park.

"Take it easy, little buddy," Jimmy yelled over his shoulder, and then he was gone, a flash of black on a bright orange skateboard, moving faster than any other skateboarder I'd ever seen move.

It took the entire bag of brownies, but Elliot finally got around to telling me what had forced him up that big tree. "I'm really sad about Lucky," he said. "I don't know why he died. He never hurt anybody."

"I don't understand it either," I admitted, wishing I had some tissues in my pocket. Elliot needed them bad. "I miss Lucky something terrible, too."

"Why would anyone kill him?" Elliot asked.

"It would have to be someone who was very sick and didn't know what he was doing," I said.

"Does Auntie Carol know who did it?" he asked.

"Not yet," I answered him. "But she'll find out and that person will be punished. He'll definitely go to jail."

"But that won't bring Lucky back," Elliot said. "I want to see Lucky again."

"I wish I could see him again, too," I said. "But I can't either. But there are some other greyhounds that I can see. And that I can help take care of until Ellen and my mom find homes for them. We need you to be strong, Elliot, so you can help us take care of the greyhounds who are still alive."

"Are they very sick now?" Elliot asked.

"I don't know," I said. "But my mom will let us know. Do you think you'll be able to come up to New Hampshire with us, maybe tomorrow or Sunday, and help us take care of the greyhounds that survived? I know that Lucky would want us to do that. He was such a great dog, Elliot." I couldn't believe it. Suddenly, I was crying. Sitting on the bench, in the freezing cold night air, holding Elliot on my lap, and bawling louder than my dirty little cousin.

"I want to go home now," Elliot said when I stopped crying. "I want to see my mommy." One look at Elliot and I knew I was dealing with a five-year-old little boy who needed his mother a lot more than he needed me.

Aunt Marcy and Uncle Bobby did their own share of crying when Elliot and I walked into their house. It's strange the way people cry when things are working out okay. But everybody in our family who saw Elliot that night cried. The policeman was the only one who didn't cry. But he was nice when he asked Elliot a whole bunch of questions. I guess Elliot gave him the right answers, because he told us all we were a very lucky family and left.

By the time I went to bed that night, I was beyond exhausted. Still, it occurred to me seconds before I fell asleep that I had forgotten to ask my mother about Boo Boo and the shelter, but I was too tired to get out of bed and find her. Besides, the truth was I just couldn't get all worked up about Boo Boo. Not that night, anyhow. It was fantastic that Elliot was back where he belonged, but things were far from perfect in our family. Aunt Marcy had gotten good news that the cancer hadn't spread, but she was due to start radiation treatments on Monday. And my mother was determined to find out who had killed Lucky. I sure didn't want little Boo Boo to be put to sleep, nor did I want Amelia to hate me, but I wasn't certain I had the power to prevent both those things from happening. There was only one thing of which I was certain. Jimmy Oliver might look like a hood, but tonight he had been a hero. I felt bad I hadn't thanked him the way I should have, but I'd get around to that. Tomorrow. Tomorrow, I would take care of everything and everybody.

Eleven

As it turned out, on Saturday my mom didn't go to New Hampshire or her shelter. Instead, she went to the animal laboratory at Morton University. "You don't have to go with me," she said when I told her I wanted to come to the lab. "I'm not going to make a scene. I just want to have a little talk with Dr. Lewis. A nice, civil little talk."

I was sorry my father wasn't there to add his two cents to the conversation. I was sure he would have managed to make her say exactly why she was going to the lab: to kill Dr. Lewis, who I was certain she was certain had killed Lucky and the two other greyhounds. But my dad had gone to the hospital for an emergency real early in the morning. He'd called a few hours later to say he'd be tied up there most of the day. The twins were running a car wash to raise money for cheerleading, and my mom and I were the only ones home.

"I want to come," I insisted, even though the animal

research lab at Morton was the last place on earth I wanted to visit. I'd been there once before and it had made me sick. It wasn't that I'd seen or heard anything to make me feel that way. It was just the knowledge of what was happening behind the closed doors of the long corridor. My mother had urged me to come and see exactly what was going on. She said it was bad, but not as bad as I imagined. Still, I had never been able to go beyond the first locked door of the department. I could never understand how anyone could bear to work in that lab.

"No, you don't want to go today," my mother answered me. She was sitting on her bed, tying her white sneakers. She always wears sneakers when she goes to the lab.

"For a quick getaway," I once commented.

"So that I'm comfortable walking through the long corridors there," she replied, but I'm sure I was right.

"No, I really do," I repeated.

"Well, then let's get out of here," she said, plunking her feet on the floor, grabbing her jacket and pocketbook, and leading the way downstairs and out the door. It was only when we were in the garage, fastening our seat belts in my mother's Volvo, that I remembered Amelia. I looked at my watch. It was ten past nine. Amelia and Boo Boo were probably just arriving at the shelter. I might have said something to my mother about Boo Boo and possibly even have asked her to make a quick stop at the shelter to check out Boo Boo if I hadn't been shocked out of my mind by someone knocking fiercely on my car window. I let go of my seat belt and looked up to see Wendy Brown peering in at me.

Immediately, my mother started the engine and opened

my window. "Can I come to the shelter with you?" Wendy asked urgently. "I tried to call you guys this morning, but your line was busy. I called Peter, but he'd already left. I really wanted to be with the dogs today, but I wasn't sure if you needed extra help or not. Is it okay if I come today, Mrs. Morgan?"

I was surprised with the way Wendy was acting. She never asked if she could come to the shelter. She just came. But today she looked shaky and uptight. "We're not going to the shelter," my mom told her. "We're going to the lab at Morton University to see Dr. Lewis and ask him a couple of questions. It's probably not a good idea for you to come with us."

"But I really want to!" Wendy said, and before my mother could say another word, Wendy was in the backseat of the car, buckling her seat belt. "I'm so upset about Lucky. Please let me come."

"You've never been there before," my mom said, looking at Wendy in her rearview mirror. "Are you sure you want to come?"

"Absolutely," Wendy insisted. I turned around to look at her. She looked a lot surer than I felt. "I promise I won't get in the way or anything. But I just can't sit around and do nothing. I really want to meet Dr. Lewis."

"I'm not even sure he's there," my mom said as she backed her car out of the garage and headed toward Boston. "But I'm like you. I can't sit around and do nothing. So I'm going to check on what's happening there and see if anybody at the lab has a clue about what happened in New Hampshire."

"I bet Dr. Lewis caused the whole thing," I said. "Why aren't the police checking it out?"

"Because they're as confused as I am," she answered. "Dr. Lewis sounded genuinely surprised when the New Hampshire police called to tell him about the massacre. He was very cooperative, they told me. I just want to ask him a few questions myself. This isn't a raid on his lab or anything like that. He's been keeping a low profile there lately. I haven't heard anything bad about him in a while. But I just have some questions about the fire and I'm hoping he can give me some answers."

"I've never even met that guy, but I hate him," Wendy said. "He has to be responsible for what happened. Who else would do such a terrible thing to greyhounds? He hates them. He hates you. I bet anything he's the one who did this."

"He's such a disgusting man," I said. "I can't believe the police aren't doing anything about him."

"No one dislikes him as much as I do," my mom said. "In the past, he's been uncooperative every time I've asked him to release a greyhound to an adoptive family. He makes me feel as if I'm the biggest pain he's ever had to deal with. But I'm just not positive he's our guy now. It would be real helpful to me if you two would just hold back your feelings and try and be as objective as possible about him. Think you can do that?"

Wendy and I both promised to be objective, but once we were in the animal research lab for five minutes, I found myself unable to be objective about anything except that I hated the animal research lab and anyone who worked there. The truth was, however, that the place didn't look the way I remembered it. Of course, I'd only been there once and that had been a good five years earlier. And I hadn't left the front entrance to the lab then. But, this time, inside the lab, I didn't see a lot of howling animals trying to scratch their way out of cages. There was plenty of yelping, but it didn't sound all that different from the kennels at my mother's shelter. Of course, the animals at my mother's shelter had a lot more to look forward to than the animals at the research lab. Maybe that was why the barking at the lab upset me so much.

Dr. Lewis, we were informed as soon as we got to the lab, was not available. His assistant Mary Long, however, was. She was new to the lab, and it was the first time my mother had ever met her. I wanted to hate her as much as I hated Dr. Lewis, but she made it very hard. She was just so pleasant and helpful.

"I'm so sorry about what happened at the greyhound farm in New Hampshire," she said to us. "I've been just sick about it. I'm sorry Paul isn't here today. He's at an animal research conference for the next two days. What can I do to help you?"

It didn't help that the woman was incredibly pretty, as well as sickeningly nice. She shook both my hand and Wendy's, as well as my mom's, and insisted on ushering the three of us into her office. In order to get there, we had to walk through the kennel area where the dogs were kept. It was a huge corridor with cement walls dividing the dogs' stalls. It looked as if the dogs were kept in separate stalls. There was a huge chain link fence surrounding the entire area, with an aluminum feeding station at each end of the fence. As we walked down the corridor, the dogs kept poking their noses out of the bars of their stalls. They were so friendly and eager to be touched that it just about broke my heart.

Wendy and I patted every nose we could. I was surprised that there were no greyhounds in the stalls. There were lots of beagles and German shepherds and labs, but not one greyhound. As soon as we got to Mary Long's office, I asked her why.

"The greyhounds aren't that good for research purposes," she explained.

"I've been saying that for years," my mother said. "But no one here ever listened to me."

"There have been a lot of changes around here, lately," Mary Long said. "One has to do with the greyhounds. They're actually too skinny and too high-strung for research purposes. Beagles are much better."

"But you don't have a beagle track nearby to supply you with fresh leftover specimens every week, do you?" my mother asked.

Mary Long kept her smile on her face, which I thought was pretty amazing, considering my mother's tone of voice. "Dr. Lewis is no longer connected with the track," she told us. "And the beagles we use are bred specifically for animal research. They're not used to any other kind of life."

"You mean, you don't just pick up the strays that no one wants at the animal shelters and experiment on them?" I asked.

"Nowadays, there's more government intervention in research labs," she answered me. "We have to conform to more stringent rules. The beagles are bred to be cooperative and they're the appropriate size for research. They're . . ."

"This is just so awful!" Wendy interrupted her. I could see the tears on her cheek. I knew how she felt. Just hearing this woman talk about cooperation and size

85

was so awful. At least, Dr. Lewis had been honest about the whole deal. The day I'd seen him he'd scowled at my mother, was disrespectful and rude when he spoke, and looked positively evil with his black mustache and permanent frown. This woman looked kind and had a gentle voice. But, still, her words were awful. "I don't see how you can bear to hurt sweet little beagles that you breed here any more than you can hurt greyhounds that are thrown away from the track," Wendy continued.

"Please, Miss Long," my mother said. "We don't mean to be rude, but you have to understand that the whole concept of animal research is painful to those of us who dedicate our lives to saving animals. I'm glad to hear that Dr. Lewis is no longer connected to the track, but we're very concerned about some recent events involving greyhounds. Perhaps, it's just not the time to be hearing about how you breed beagles to be cooperative. I appreciate your giving us your time, but we came here for another reason."

Mary Long sighed and offered my mother yet another of her unlimited supply of smiles. "And that reason is to see if Paul Lewis had anything to do with the tragic deaths of the greyhounds in New Hampshire. Correct?"

"I appreciate your frankness," my mother said. "Yes, that's the reason."

"Well, I can assure you he did not," Mary Long said. "Personally, I know exactly where he was on Wednesday evening. He was with me at a private function."

My mother gave her a strange smile and then she shook her head. "Ah, I see. I'd heard he was getting married again. You're his fianceé, aren't you?"

"Yes, I am," Mary Long said. "But I'm also a researcher at the animal lab here. I have a doctorate in biology and specialize in cancer drug research."

Suddenly, my mother's face turned pasty white. It was as if Mary Long had slapped her. "I see," my mother finally said, and I wasn't at all certain what she saw, except that it had to be something that surprised her. I didn't think it was such a big deal that Mary Long was engaged to Dr. Lewis. Except that explained why she would lie about his whereabouts. But my mom looked real weak, like all her energy had suddenly been turned off. "Is there anything else you can tell us about the greyhound incident?" she continued, her voice sounding weaker than before. "Any suggestions about where we might look to find the real culprits, since Dr. Lewis is obviously not the one we're looking for?"

"I wish I could help you," Mary Long answered, "but I'm as confused as you. I hope you might be able to understand that I love animals deeply and that I work very hard here to make certain none of them suffer unnecessarily."

"That's gibberish," Wendy said angrily. "Every time you touch one of these animals, you hurt him."

"Not exactly," Mary Long said, keeping her voice low and calm. "If we give them injections, we do it as gently and quickly as possible."

"Oh, that's great," Wendy said. "You give them a shot gently and then torture them till they die."

"They don't all die," Mary Long insisted. "Many of them are cured with the drugs we're testing."

"But you give them all cancer, don't you?" I asked.

"Not all of them," she answered me. "But I'm not going to lie to you. Many of them do contract the disease, and we work hard to cure them. We give them lots of love and walk them regularly and feed them well. We never purposefully or needlessly hurt any of these animals. But they are here for a purpose.''

''And could that purpose be to find a cure for breast cancer?'' my mother asked softly.

Mary Long looked at her for a long moment before she answered. ''Yes, it is,'' she finally said.

''You give these poor little beagles breast cancer!?'' Wendy asked, horrified. ''I can't believe you would do that.''

Mary Long's perpetual smile finally began to fade. ''I know that sounds horrible,'' she began, ''but . . .''

''But sometimes human lives are more important than animal lives,'' my mother answered for Mary Long. She looked directly at Wendy. ''Believe me, no one loves animals as much as I do. I work every day of my life to provide them with decent, loving homes so they can lead healthy love-filled lives. Sometimes, I feel as if every greyhound that is mistreated is my fault. I wish I had enough power so that I could prevent the way they're treated at the track. But I'm just one person and I have my limits. But what Dr. Long is doing here is every bit as important as what's happening at my shelter. Probably, it's more important, because she's saving human lives and I'm just saving animal lives. It hurts me deeply to use those words, 'just saving animal lives,' but it's true, Wendy.''

I'd never heard my mother sound like that. She was always so upbeat and positive about what she did. But I wasn't stupid. I knew what was going on in her mind. It was Aunt Marcy who was pushing her into this new attitude. I looked through the window on Dr. Long's office door and I could see the long corridor filled with cages. I wanted to grab every beagle and German shepherd and Labrador retriever that was locked up in his cage. I wanted to release every animal so he could run happily through the nearby parks and fields. I wanted him to be free of needles and painful procedures. I wanted him to sleep on his master's bed and eat in his own feeding dish in his master's kitchen. But I also wanted Aunt Marcy to be free of the breast cancer that Dr. Long was injecting into each of these dogs. I wanted her to live. I was used to making bargains with God. I do it all the time. I'd have given up my spot on the basketball team if she could have been free of the disease, but God hadn't gone along with that idea. Now I'd give up every one of these adorable beagles so that she could watch Elliot grow up and *The Simpsons* with me.

"Thank you for seeing us," my mom said to Dr. Long as the three of us started to walk out of her office. Wendy looked ready to cry again and looked even more confused than when she'd buckled herself into our Volvo. My mother was smiling, but it was a shaky smile. I couldn't bear the thought of the little black snouts sticking out of the cages, hoping for the quick touch of my fingers. But the three of us walked down that long corridor and touched as many snouts as we could. It was the least we could do.

Twelve

Peter Chandler was taking shots at the hoop attached to my garage when we got home. "Where you guys been?" he asked when Wendy and I walked over to the net. "We waited at the shelter for you all morning."

Wendy grabbed the ball, did a quick dribble, and sank the shot. I'd forgotten what a good player she was. Real often last summer, she and Jessica had gone two on two with me and Peter and had given us a good game. A couple of times, Wendy had come over alone and Jimmy had joined her against me and Peter. The two of them had taken us to the hole plenty of times. Both girls had decided to go out for cheerleading instead of basketball this year, but Wendy had said that maybe next year she'd try out for the girls' hoop team. I grabbed her rebound and the three of us went at it pretty strong for a good fifteen minutes. Finally, exhausted and sweaty, we all sat down on the railroad ties at the end of the driveway. "So where were you, anyhow?" Peter asked again.

"We went to the Morton lab with my mom to see Dr. Lewis," I answered him.

"Wow!" Peter said. "That must have been some scene. Did your mom level him?"

"He wasn't there," Wendy answered. "The only one we talked to was his girlfriend. She tried to make us believe everything they do at the lab is sweet and gentle. It's all fun and games there. According to her, she and Dr. Lewis and the dogs all have one big party going on there."

"Come off it, Wendy," I said. "They do important research there."

"On how to make dogs miserable?" Peter asked.

"On how to cure breast cancer," I added. "My Aunt Marcy has breast cancer, you know."

Wendy looked like I'd smacked her in the stomach. "Oh, my God," she gasped. "No wonder your mom went off about the importance of research. Man, I'm sorry, Benjy. I didn't know that. Was that why Elliot ran away last night? I thought it was because of the greyhounds."

"It was both things," I said.

"Man, that's tough," Peter said. "Your aunt is so cool. But I've got to tell you, Benjy. Amelia wasn't the least bit cool this morning. She was on fire."

"I know," I sighed. "I forgot to tell my mom about Boo Boo. What happened?"

"The dog bit both Sheryl and Allison. Bad."

"That dog should be given to Dr. Lewis," Wendy said. "I'll bring it there personally."

"Was Amelia real pissed at me for not showing?" I asked.

"That's putting it mildly," he said. "She called your

house at least three times. I'll tell you one thing, though.'' He shook his head and smiled. ''She sure is pretty when she's mad.''

''You know something?'' Wendy asked. ''Now that I think about it, she's really just your type, Peter. You two would look great together.''

''Look, you two,'' I said, standing up, ''I've got to go speak to my mom about the dog now. It's the least I can do for poor Amelia.''

''Oh, don't waste your breath,'' Peter said. ''The dog's dead meat. Sheryl said they'd never keep a dog that vicious at the shelter. She said it should be put to sleep. Actually, after Amelia left in a big huff, Sheryl suggested Amelia be put to sleep, too. ''

''Great,'' I moaned as Wendy roared with laughter. ''I can hardly wait to see her on Monday.''

I hadn't even gotten into the garage when I heard my mom's car came flying out. ''I'm going to the shelter for an hour,'' she told us as she backed out of the driveway. ''Then I'm going to New Hampshire. Aunt Marcy invited you all over for dinner. She says Elliot's still upset and needs the company. Call her and tell her when you're coming.'' She stopped the car for a second and then added, ''You're all invited.''

''Can we come to New Hampshire with you?'' Wendy asked. ''I'd be glad to do anything you wanted up there. Anything at all.''

''Thanks, but no thanks,'' my mother said. ''Ellen needs me to speak to the police. She's worn out. Just stay here and do what you can with Elliot. He needs cheering up.'' She took off and then stopped again. ''Oh, Benjy,'' she yelled through her car window. ''Sheryl says some girl from your class brought a vicious little dog to the shelter. She had some mouth on her. Who is she, anyhow?''

"Just some girl in my homeroom,'' I said. "But I feel bad for the dog.''

"I feel bad for a lot of dogs,'' my mother said. "But, like you saw this morning, I can't save every one of them.'' And then she was gone. Peter had to take off, so Wendy and I played one on one. I was on fire, but Wendy wiped the floor with me. When our game finally ended, I should have been frustrated with my loss. But I wasn't. For the first time all day, I actually felt good. Good enough to walk over to Aunt Marcy's with Wendy and take Elliot to the park.

"She just killed me shooting hoops,'' I told Elliot as Wendy and I pushed him on the swings. "I was Bird. But she was Kareem. And she pinned me to the boards.''

Elliot squealed with delight as Wendy danced around in front of his swing, pretending to be knocked to the ground every time his sneakers touched her jeans. "I'm Superwoman!'' Wendy shouted as she sprang back up to a standing position the second the swing hurtled back toward me. "No mere puny little mortal can keep me down.''

"Are you two boyfriend and girlfriend?'' Elliot asked when we finally stopped the swing and sat down on the grass.

"No way!'' Wendy answered immediately. "He's got the hots for a paper girl with a savage mop for a dog.''

"Is that right?'' Elliot asked me.

"No way,'' I said as I tied his right sneaker. Then I leaned forward and whispered in his ear, "I'm swearing off all women for the rest of my life. They're nothing but trouble.''

While Wendy remained collapsed on the grass, I put Elliot back in the swing and pushed him evenly and smoothly toward the sky. "She isn't prettier than the paper girl," Elliot told me as I pulled his swing backward. "But she's got much better legs."

The kid, I knew for sure, was five years old, but man who would ever believe it?

Thirteen

Aunt Marcy and Uncle Bobby ended up taking Elliot out for supper, so the twins made Dad and me omelets for dinner. They made my father's and mine with cheese and tomatoes. They both know I hate tomatoes, but I decided to simply eat the stupid thing and not cause a fuss. That was not my usual way, but I was pretty worn out from my day's activities and just not up to a battle with the twin witches.

"We saw your stupid assistant basketball coach," Jillian said when she sat down and started to eat her peanut-butter-and-raisin omelet. I have never seen a more disgusting omelet than a peanut-butter-and-raisin omelet. Except for the banana and prune concoction Jenny was wolfing down.

"Oh, yeah," I said, trying to act like it was no big deal if she saw Will Sheridan, but dropping dead inside at the possibility of my sisters saying something to him about what an awful player I was. "Where?"

"He came to the car wash we ran for the basketball team," Jenny said. She always answers the questions I ask Jillian. "He brought his cute little red Volkswagen through twice."

"That was nice of him," my father said. "Did you tell him you were Benjy's sisters?"

"We didn't have to," Jillian said. She always answers Jenny's questions. It sounds weird, but you get used to it. "He already knows that. Actually, Dad, in case you didn't know this, that's the only reason Benjy's on the team. This guy has a thing for me and Jenny."

"Are you serious?" my father asked, looking horrified. "That's not the least bit amusing. How old is this guy, anyhow?"

"Not that old," Jenny said. "He's a junior. I feel bad because I hate to see Benjy dumped off the team, but I betcha anything that's going to happen."

I couldn't eat another mouthful of my cheese-and-tomato omelet. It was bad enough that Amelia Parker had probably taken out a contract on my life, but my own sisters were holding a knife to my throat. My whole life could be destroyed by girls who hated me. "What do you mean?" I asked, giving up the disinterested pose. What was the sense? The twins knew how I felt. There was nowhere I could hide on this one.

"Well," Jillian began, pausing for this dramatic effect that made me want to pick up her peanut-butter-and-raisin omelet and dump it all over her blond head. "It's not a pretty picture, but that Will guy came over to me and Jenny after the second time he drove his car through our squad of washers and started to be real friendly."

She paused again, kind of dangling her fork in the

air for some stupid effect. This time, she knocked my dad over the edge. "Will you get to the point already, Jillian?" he asked impatiently. "Enough playing around with Benjy's feelings. What exactly did this guy say to you?"

"Okay," Jenny continued. "Here goes. He said, 'Where did you two learn to give such a great car wash?' And when we both just kind of smiled and shrugged, he said, 'Can I hire you two great car washers to come over every Saturday night to clean my car?' We both just smiled again. I mean, what could you say to a dumb question like that? Then, he said, 'Well, maybe Benjy can get you to do a little favor for his assistant coach.' So, I said, 'Maybe Benjy can wash your car for you.' Then he said, 'I think Benjy's too busy practicing his basketball shots to have time to do that.' And then Jillian said, 'We have to get back to work,' and he just sort of smiled real funny at us and left."

When Jenny stopped talking, my father had the same confused look on his face that I was certain was on mine. "Is that it?" he finally asked.

"Yup," Jillian said. "But you sort of had to be there to understand exactly what the guy was saying. I'm telling you, Dad, he was coming on to me and Jenny. It was gross."

My father sighed and put down his fork. He'd only eaten a few bites of his omelet, but he sure didn't look hungry. "I don't know what to say," he said, which was a pretty unusual thing for my father to say, since he always knows what to say. "You're accusing this kid of some kind of sexual harassment and that's a pretty big accusation. It's hard to tell from his words exactly what he was saying. But I trust both your judgments, and if that's what you believe, then that's the way it is. If he's making you uncomfortable, that's a problem."

"But they don't have to be around him," I said. "They don't ever have to come to another one of my practices or to any of my games. Actually, I think it's a terrific idea for them to stay away from me and my basketball team for the whole season."

"Oh, you're just so smart," Jenny said nastily. "If Jillian and I stay away from you and your precious team, you're off the team, buddy."

"That's the truth," Jillian added, just in case I didn't already know it. "You're a crummy player and shouldn't have been on the team in the first place. You should have seen him at tryouts, Dad. It was a joke. He couldn't get the ball in the basket if someone picked him up and carried him up to the rim. Now, he has a choice. He can stay on the team and wait for Mr. Murray and Will Sheridan to throw him off, or he can drop out and save all of us a lot of embarrassment."

It's funny. I've been living with these brats for twelve years, and I've always known they can't stand me as much as I can't stand them. But, sometimes, like at that moment, it still comes as a shock that they can hate me so much. Still, as unlucky as I am to have been born into the same family as the two of them, I did have a little bit of luck when our father turned out to be a psychiatrist who every now and then is on the mark.

"You know, girls," he said while I sat there, open-mouthed and in my Amelia Parker mode of muteness, "unless I'm mistaken here, I seem to be picking up some very disturbing vibes. Like it's not just a simple case of you two trying to report an unpleasant scene, but rather an example of you both trying to make your brother's life miserable. I have no way of knowing if Benjy made the team because he can play basketball or because the assistant coach has an eye for his sisters. All I know is that he flirted with you at a car wash and even though you'd probably never report that incident, you feel it's grounds for Benjy to drop off the team. I'm not so sure you're correct in that particular assumption. I can tell you, however, that it bothers me that an assistant coach would shamelessly flirt with the sisters of one of his players and act like he expects favors from them. But it infuriates me that my daughters are tormenting my son."

Jillian and Jenny looked plenty nervous. It's not very often that our dad sounds the way he did at that moment, which was ready to hand out a lengthy grounding. Most of the time the three of us don't pay all that much attention to his lengthy lectures, because they're so frequent and boring, but this time he had all three of us.

At that moment, I for one could understand why our dad had been written up in *Boston Magazine* as one of the top psychiatrists in the greater Boston area. "I suggest you two girls give this matter a little bit more thought," the famous shrink continued. "If you still think that the assistant coach was flirting with you in a suggestive manner and you would be willing to discuss his attitude with him and your principal, I would have no problem setting up such an interview. Of course, I would certainly be present at this meeting to defend you both in any way I could. But if you decide that you're not willing to take that step, then I suggest you bury this matter and stay away from this Will Sheridan. And

I also might suggest that the two of you analyze why you harbor such negative feelings toward your younger brother. I for one do not think it appropriate behavior for two fifteen-year-old girls to go so out of their way to be nasty to a twelve-year-old boy. I would think they would both have much more important things to do with their time and energies."

There was a long silence at the table while the four of us picked at what was left of our four cold omelets. Finally, I broke the silence. I was just so sick of being struck mute whenever I needed to speak in my own defense. I'd never been that way before I noticed Amelia Parker, and I had no intention of becoming permanently soundless. "I'm not a great basketball player," I said to the three of them. "I'm not bad in front of my own hoop, but when I get into a game situation at the school gym, I suck. I'm sure Mr. Murray put me on the team because Will Sheridan thought the twins were good-looking. I'll probably drop off the team on Monday."

"That's your decision," my father said. "But you better give it some more thought."

"Why?" I asked him, waiting for my sisters to start to smirk. So far, they had two perfectly blank, identical faces. "You don't think that's a good decision? Someone knows he stinks and he gets off the team. That makes perfect sense to me."

"I think it might be the easy way out of a difficult situation," he said. "And you know how I feel about easy ways out."

I picked up my plate and carried it over to the sink, where I dumped out the big portion of my omelet that was still sitting there. I wished I could have come up with a great line, something to let my sisters know they had hurt me deeply, but I was a better person than they'd ever be, and I could hurt them wicked bad if I wanted to, but I just wasn't in the mood for any more games. Besides, Peter and Johnny Simons were coming over with a new Nintendo game and I had to get myself out of my black mood. "There are more important things than a stupid sixth-grade basketball team," I told the three of them, and I left the kitchen, wishing I could believe such an idiotic statement.

Three hours later I was pretty close to winning my first game of Dragons when my mother came home from New Hampshire. Accompanied by three greyhounds, one of which was such a dead ringer for Lucky that I dropped my remote and continued my perfect record of losing every game I'd played that entire day.

Fourteen

The next few hours were wild. "All I know," my mother explained as the five of us ran around trying to feed, walk, wash, and relax the poor dogs, "is that a few minutes after I got to Ellen's, the phone rang and a male voice told Ellen there were three greyhounds in a cage at the entrance to the farm. Then he hung up, and we raced outside and, sure enough, there were these three beauties, all jammed into one big cage, sitting there, looking at us.

"You know how nuts Ellen is. In two seconds, she was all over the dogs, hugging and kissing them, naming each one immediately. They're Jo-Jo, Cerce, and Caesar. But the poor woman is so overwhelmed with the results of the fire. My God, her whole barn was destroyed. How could I leave these three dogs there? She's having enough trouble taking care of the eight healthy greyhounds that survived the fire. Her neighbors and friends are already building her a new barn, but she's keeping

102

the eight dogs in her house. And she's putting the finishing touches on three adoptions. It won't be long until she has her remaining dogs out of the house and in the barn. But, still, she couldn't possibly handle these three. So, here they are.''

My mother was talking so fast it was hard to understand her. My father, who certainly didn't need to go to the hospital for his share of crazies that night, convinced her to sit down and let the four of us take care of the dogs. His calmness and kindness were pretty good signs that he was worried about my mother. One thing my father does not enjoy is having my mother's dogs stay in our house. He's always willing to go to the shelter to help out when she needs him there, but having stray dogs in our house ticks him off. Anyhow, that night he sent me and the twins out to take the dogs for a long walk to try and relax them before we fed them and cleaned them up.

I grabbed Cerce, Lucky's look-alike. It was amazing how much Cerce resembled Lucky. They were both black and white with four white paws and a black tail that ended in a white triangle. Their ears were both black, rimmed with white, and their brown eyes had speckles around the irises. It was enough to make me nuts. Even Jillian noticed the resemblance. ''Hey, that dog could be Lucky's brother,'' she announced as we took off for our walk.

I wasn't anxious to walk with the twin witches, but it was pretty late at night, and Johnny and Peter were long gone. Plus, I saw no reason to let my hatred for my sisters make me an easy prey for some Saturday night drunk who was hiding behind the bushes, waiting to slice me up with his pocket knife.

"Yeah," Jenny added. "They look more alike than me and Jillian."

"And they're a lot better-looking," I said. I needed to walk with them to stay alive, but I didn't want any misunderstanding that I could stand either one of them.

"But Lucky was fatter," Jillian said. "I've never seen such a skinny dog as this one. I don't remember Lucky being that scrawny."

I couldn't help it. I'd talk about Lucky with anyone at this point. "He wasn't scrawny," I agreed. "Lucky probably weighed three pounds more than Cerce. And he didn't have the overbite this dog has. Lucky's teeth were perfectly straight. And he had great gums. But other than that, these two are amazingly identical."

"Where did Lucky come from anyhow?" Jenny asked. "I can't remember."

"He was one of Dr. Lewis's rejects," I reminded her. "Mom got him on one of her roundups there. Remember, she got the night janitor to let her in one night when it was real rainy and she grabbed Lucky and brought him right to our house. He was soaking wet when I first saw him. And he was so skittish. Mom said it was because of the drugs he'd been given. He wouldn't walk the stairs for weeks. He was real weak from the drugs. But he was so smart. All you'd have to do is tell him something once, and he did it for life. Like the way he'd get the paper from the family room and bring it into the kitchen for Dad. And how good he was with Elliot. Elliot was real little then, but Lucky would shake with pleasure every time he saw him. He'd fetch that ball for Elliot for hours."

While I was talking, Cerce was walking so close to my leg, I was having trouble walking. It was like I had three legs. I bent down and patted his head. He looked up at me with such sweet, sad eyes that for a second I felt a lump in my throat. That was all I needed to do: Cry in front of the twins.

"Yeah, I liked that dog," Jenny said, unaware that her brother was biting the insides of his mouth to keep from crying. "He used to bring my hairbrush into my bedroom from the bathroom when I asked him to. I wish we'd adopted him and then he'd still be alive."

"Mom wanted to keep him," Jillian said. "But Dad refused."

I remembered that well. I'd been heartbroken when Dad had opposed Mom's request. But he'd been adamant. Even though he hated it, Mom could bring home animals if the shelter was filled, but none of them could stay permanently. That was his big rule. No matter how much he disliked strays in our house temporarily, it was important that we always have room for them. Dogs of our own would complicate things. I disagreed with him, but there was nothing I could do about it. I love having dogs stay with us for a month or so at a time. But it does make our house confusing. I guess my father has to have some say in the animal situation or my mother would fill every room with a dozen permanent new additions to our house. But Lucky had been so special. If only we'd broken that rule and kept him.

"I bet you anything Dr. Lewis was behind the fire," Jenny said as we headed back toward our house. I'd been so lost in thought about Lucky that I hadn't even noticed that Cerce was still attached to my right side. It wasn't that easy to walk with a greyhound fastened to your leg. "He was furious about Lucky and figured he'd get him back one way or the other. He was just waiting for the right opportunity.''

"I don't know," I said. "I thought so, too, but after going to the lab this morning, I'm not so sure. His assistant was so nice. They're going to get married. She says they need to use animals to find cures for diseases like cancer. And she says they're not using many grey-hounds anymore.''

"For cancer?" Jillian said. "Are they finding cures for breast cancer now?''

"They're working on it," I said.

"Yeah, but why do they have to kill the animals?" Jenny asked. "Can't they just work on rats or mice? Why dogs?''

"I don't know," I admitted. "But now that Aunt Marcy is sick, it sure makes you wonder about the whole thing.''

"I'm real worried about her," Jillian said. "Just before we left, I heard Mom talking to her on the phone. It sounded like Aunt Marcy was a basket case. Mom kept saying, 'I promise you it will be all right. You just have to be strong.' Aunt Marcy always seems so strong. I don't know what I would do if she dies.''

"She's not going to die," I said. I had no idea why I said that. I knew absolutely nothing about her case. "A dog might have to die, but she won't.''

"That's gross, Benjy," Jenny said, and I had to agree. Cerce was licking my hand when I patted his head. It was as if he'd heard me and was licking me the way Lucky used to when I had to hurt him while I was brushing or pulling fleas off of him. Man, had that dog been something.

"Real gross," Jillian agreed. "You're sick, Benjy."

I shrugged my shoulders and continued to let Cerce lick my hand. For once, my sisters were right. I was sick. But, I was afraid I was also right. Some dog in some lab was going to have to die so people like our aunt could live.

The next night we went to Aunt Marcy's for dinner and *The Simpsons*. Mom tried to get her to come to our house instead, but she refused. And she insisted that we bring the dogs with us. All three of them.

Elliot was reading in his room when we came in. "He's been there all day," Uncle Bobby told me. "I couldn't get him out of here. I tried everything. He won't talk to your father. He wouldn't even go golfing with me. He knows Marcy's going in for chemotherapy tomorrow and it's got him all upset. Maybe you can talk to him."

Elliot put down his book when I walked in. He was reading *The Three Little Pigs and the Hungry Wolf*. I don't think Elliot can really read, but he's heard the story so many times that he knows the words by heart.

"So, want to come down for dinner, buddy?" I asked him as I sat down on the bed beside him.

"No thanks," he said. "My mom said you have a surprise for me. What is it?"

"It's downstairs," I said. Actually, I was a little nervous about showing Elliot a dog who looked exactly like Lucky. I was worried that it would confuse him. My father had said that Elliot was mature enough to understand that Lucky was dead and Cerce just resembled him, but I wasn't so sure. "Want to come down and see a dog who looks exactly like Lucky? His name is Cerce and he's a little younger than Lucky, but the two of them could have been brothers."

Elliot put his book down and stared at me. "Lucky is dead," he said solemnly.

"He is," I answered.

"He's real dead. Like Simba's father. Not like Snow White."

" 'Fraid so," I said.

"I hate it when things die," he said.

"I don't like it either," I said.

"People die. Not just animals," he told me.

"They do," I agreed.

"I just hope Mommy doesn't die," he said.

"She won't," I told him. "She's going to get some medicine to make her well. It might make her a little sick at the beginning, but then it will make her well. You wait and see. I promise. Come down and meet Cerce. You're going to love him."

"No, I'm not," he said. "I loved Lucky. He was a great dog. But I don't even know Cerce. Just 'cause he looks like someone I loved doesn't mean I have to love him."

Man, could I have used my father here. I thought I understood what Elliot was trying to say, which might have been that if his mother died, he wasn't going to love some other mother just because she looked like his mom. What kind of five-year-old thinks like that? It's amazing. But that's Elliot. I just hoped he wasn't planning to run away again.

"Okay," I said. "You don't have to love Cerce. But it sure would help if you were nice to him. You see, we don't know where these three dogs came from. They were just put on Ellen's doorstep. You know, the way so many cats and dogs end up at my mom's shelter. But these dogs really need love. All three of them. Caesar and Jo-Jo, too. This time, I could use your help. Okay?''

Elliot didn't say anything for a while. He just lay back on his bed and stared at his ceiling. He's got these neat clouds painted on his blue ceiling, so it looks like you're staring at the sky. I lay down beside him and stared up at the ceiling, too. I'd almost fallen asleep when Elliot tugged at my arm. He was sitting up and looking down at me. "Don't you think it would be a good idea if these dogs could just run away?" he asked me in a very serious voice.

I was confused for a minute, but I snapped myself awake. "Jo-Jo, Cerce, and Caesar?" I asked.

"Yes," he answered me.

I waited a minute before I replied. I knew Elliot pretty well and I understood that this mind was sometimes a little hard to follow. His body might be five years old, but his mind was close to a hundred. "A good idea for who?" I asked him. "The dogs or us?"

"Everybody," he answered.

Then it hit me. "Oh, I see what you're saying," I said. "It would be easier for the dogs because they wouldn't have to worry about fires in their barn. Or experiments. And it would be easier for us because we wouldn't have to worry about losing the dogs some-day." He nodded. For a minute, I thought about talking to Elliot about what Dr. Long had told us about experiments on dogs and cures for cancer, but I dropped that idea. "Yeah," I finally began, choosing my words real carefully, "it might be a lot easier for dogs to run away. But I don't think the dogs would like it. I think they'd be lonely and hungry out there by themselves. It's hard to love somebody that you might lose. It was awful for

Simba. But he got through it and he became king. I miss Lucky something awful, Elliot. But I'm glad he was my friend for the time I knew him.''

I was catching my breath, trying to figure out how to drive home my point about kids solving nothing by running away when Elliot stood up, stretched his arms, and announced he was going downstairs. "I'm hungry," he said as he headed out his bedroom door. "I hope Mom put lots of onions in my hamburger." I closed my mouth and followed him downstairs.

Aunt Marcy looked a little bit tired, but other than that, not much different than she did every Sunday evening before eight o'clock. She was wearing her blue Marge wig and had made the twins wear their wigs, too. She loved to make the twins up as Marge's hideous sisters, complete with beer cans (empty, of course, or my mother would have hit the roof) and chocolate cigarettes. Aunt Marcy looked terrific and was her usual pre-Simpson excited self. She was frying us Simpson burgers and had even bought us slush. She gave Elliot a big hug and a plate filled with potato chips and a hamburger. "Where are the dogs?" he asked her.

"In the yard," she said. "Want to give them some burgers?"

Elliot nodded, put three more burgers on his plate, and headed outside to the yard, where the three dogs were playing with each other. Man, did they seem happy to be outside and free. A fenced-in yard is heaven to them.

All three dogs rushed Elliot the minute they saw him. I don't know what it is about little kids, but greyhounds love them. I've seen other breeds that are nervous around little kids, but never greyhounds. Jo-Jo and Caesar sniffed and licked him fiercely, but Cerce just stood to one side and stared at him. Elliot let the dogs lick him, smiling and giggling over their attention. It took a few minutes until he noticed Cerce. His eyes opened real wide and his mouth just kind of dropped open. "Wow," he said. "Wow."

"I told you, didn't I?" I said. I was worried about him. He looked so fragile. Maybe my dad should have come outside with us. "What a resemblance, huh?"

Elliot walked over to Cerce, who seemed shyer around Elliot than he'd been around me and the twins. "Hey, boy," Elliot said, but Cerce stood still, locked in his spot. Elliot broke off a piece of hamburger and put it in his outstretched hand. "Here, Cerce," he said gently. The other two dogs swarmed around Elliot, but he held his ground. "This is for you, Cerce," he said. "Come and get it."

I took the other two hamburgers off Elliot's plate and busied myself feeding the other two dogs while Elliot and Cerce stared at one another. Jo-Jo and Caesar had wolfed down every last piece of the hamburger before Cerce finally approached Elliot. Before he took the piece of hamburger, Cerce licked Elliot's hand thoroughly, almost as if he were a mother cat washing off her newborn kitty. Next thing I knew, Elliot was sprawled out on the ground, howling with delight, while Cerce licked his face with the same intensity he had devoted to his hand. It was funny, I thought as I watched the scene in front of me, Lucky had been the most affectionate animal I'd ever met, but this Cerce had him beat by a mile.

Fifteen

Dr. Lewis stopped by our house early Monday morning. I had just come downstairs for breakfast and my mother had already left for the shelter. I wanted to throw up when I opened the front door and saw him standing there. I was already in pretty bad shape about the day. Facing Amelia Parker and Coach Murray was not going to be fun. The last thing I needed to begin this tough day with was a visit from one of the people I hated most in the entire world.

"My mother's not here," I told him in my nastiest voice. Jo-Jo, Caesar, and Cerce had gathered around him and begun their serious sniffing routine. It made me plenty nervous to have this guy see these dogs. After all, he was a greyhound murderer. It was getting to be a common occurrence that when I needed my parents, they were nowhere around. Man, my dad is a psychiatrist and my mother runs an animal shelter, but when I'm facing a distraught five-year-old or a notorious dog torturer, where are they? Helping other people's kids and other people's dogs. "She's at her shelter. Taking care of neglected and mistreated animals."

"So, are you Benjy Morgan?" he asked, bending down and offering the top of his hand to the three dogs for an introductory smell, acting more pleasant than I wanted him to be. When you dislike someone, it confuses everything when he turns out to be nice. Even for a fleeting moment.

"Yes," I answered, surprised both by his gesture to the dogs and by the fact that he knew my name. "And I've got to get to school now. I'm real late."

"Of course," he said in that same annoyingly nice tone. "I'll just head out of here and see if I can find your mother at her shelter." He turned around and was just about out the door when he stopped and turned back toward me. Man, was my luck ever going to turn good or was I doomed forever? "I just wanted to tell you that Dr. Long was very impressed with you on Saturday," he continued. "I'm sorry I missed you and your mother and your friend. I wanted to answer your mother's questions as soon and as completely as I could. I know you're all very upset about the fire. I am, too."

"You couldn't be," I said. I saw no reason to act differently than I felt. This man might be acting nice, but he couldn't fool me "You caused it all."

"I know it must sound that way to you," he said, "but that's not the way it is. I'd like to explain this to your mother, Benjy. But let me say it first to you. I had nothing to do with that fire and I deeply regret that it happened. Whoever set it should be prosecuted to the full degree of the law. I will do anything I can to find that person and make sure he is punished. What he did is unconscionable.''

It was getting very late. I needed to leave my house immediately or I would be late for homeroom, but something stopped me from slamming the door in the face of this short man with the dark suit and the big mustache that covered his whole top lip and the bottom of his nose. Maybe it was the fact that Cerce was attached to my leg again, and I could feel the cool tip of his nose right through my jeans. ''It's no worse than what you do every day in your lab,'' I said while I patted Cerce's smooth head. Jo-Jo and Caesar were leaning against Dr. Lewis. Couldn't they tell how dangerous this man was for greyhounds? Any second, I expected him to grab a couple of leashes and tie them around the dogs' necks. But he'd never get away with that in my house. I'd tackle him and knock him to the ground before he laid a finger on one of these innocent dogs. ''I remember how awful you were to my mother when she tried to get some greyhounds out of your lab. You practically had her arrested.''

''She was breaking the law,'' he said. ''I know it's hard for you to understand what happens in my lab. You see me as an ogre who tortures dogs mercilessly. I know that's how I often seem. Dr. Long has worked hard trying to get me to be more compassionate, but the truth is, Benjy, I really can't be.''

There was something in this man's voice that made me decide to be late for school. Big deal. I'd miss Amelia in homeroom. She'd find me later. Her and Coach Murray. ''I don't understand what you're saying,'' I said, but I had a funny feeling that I did. I just needed him to explain it more fully.

"That's because I don't completely understand it myself," he said. "I'm a veterinarian, Benjy. I was trained to save the lives of animals. Yet somewhere along the way I got involved in animal research. My role changed. Suddenly, I was trying to save human lives by experimenting on animals. The only way I could make that switch was to stop caring about every animal that came into my lab. They were all numbers. Nothing more. That worked for me. I've done some very important work in the field of allergy research because of my experiments on animals. Allergy research may not seem like something very important. But I can assure you there are thousands of sick people whose lives were made bearable because of the medications I helped develop for them through animal experimentation. A year ago, Dr. Long came into my lab and I began to work with her on cancer research. She's a brilliant woman. But, more importantly, she's a compassionate woman. It hurts to care about animals that you know might die. I always believed that caring could hinder my effectiveness as a researcher. But Dr. Long taught me that kind of thinking is not always true."

He stopped talking and I stopped rubbing Cerce's head. I'd heard more than I wanted to. It was important to me that I detest Dr. Lewis and everything that happened in his lab. Dr. Long was different. I knew she hurt animals, but I knew it hurt her to do that. Besides, she was helping people like Aunt Marcy fight cancer. Dr. Lewis was the enemy. I'd hated him for years. He'd practically killed Lucky three years ago, and I was sure he'd finished the job three days ago. "I have to go to school," I said simply, my hand on the front door.

"And I wish you wouldn't go to my mother's shelter. You can call her from here if you want."

"Don't worry," he said. "I'm not going to cause her any trouble. I just want to share my thoughts on the fire with her. I have some ideas about just who might have set that fire. It's no easier for me to go to her shelter than it is for you to come to my lab. I wish every dog I treated could go to the shelter and be provided with a loving family. But I also wish all the diseases in the world would just go away. Bye, Benjy."

He bent down and patted all three of the dogs. When Cerce licked his hand, Dr. Lewis glanced up at me, and I swear his eyes looked real funny. I watched him get in his car and drive away before I put the three dogs in the screened-in porch off the kitchen and took off for school. Was there anything in my life these days, I wondered as I rode my bicycle down the street, that was simple?

Amelia Parker answered that question with a resounding, "No!" Ms. Evans readily accepted my excuse about being late. She was a real animal lover and knew all about the fire and my mother's shelter. As soon as I started to tell her about the three new greyhounds I'd had to walk that morning, she stopped me. "Your mother is the most amazing woman I know," she said while I gathered up my books and headed out the door to English. "I swear, Benjy, I sleep better at nights knowing she's out there helping the strays." I gave her my most sincere smile and had an excellent chance of making it to English on time when Amelia found me.

"Well, there you are!" she announced, standing in front of me, her hands on her hips. "I wondered when you'd finally show up. I hope you told your mother Boo Boo and I will be coming to the shelter this afternoon.''

I nodded. No matter what craziness was going on in my life, Amelia was a rock of stability. Around her, nothing changed. I was a mute. "Well, that's good," she said. "Because Boo Boo cannot be home when my father gets home from his trip tonight. His life is in your hands, Benjy."

I nodded again. That was good news. Not only did I have to worry about every greyhound and beagle that might be sacrificed for medical research, now I had Boo Boo's blood on my hands, too. "I'll see you after school," Amelia informed me before she turned around and ran down the corridor to her class. She was wearing a real short skirt and her legs were even longer than I'd remembered. I'd seen those legs bicycle up to my front walk dozens of times, but I hadn't realized until that moment how long they were. The girl was making me mute and crazy with her demands about her demented dog, but I couldn't help getting swept away by her. She was just so good-looking. I did wish I had some control of my voice so I could have told her that I had to go to basketball practice after school so that Coach Murray could throw me off the team. But I figured that whole scene would probably only take two minutes, so how late could I be?

Very late, I learned the minute practice began. Will Sheridan had apparently decided that having Coach Murray throw me off the team was too soft a punishment for the twins' rejection. Instead, he would, following the twins' example, torture me slowly and mercilessly. For two solid hours, he concentrated only on me, running me up and down the court, giving me ''special'' drills to make my legs move "faster than your usual dead snail pace," interrupting this constructive criticism with push-ups and sit-ups. While the rest of the team played ball, I was slowly and painstakingly deflated till I was nothing more than a flattened basketball.

Midway through this torment, right in the middle of an endless string of push-ups, I decided to give up. What was I trying to prove anyhow? The coach hated me. I was a lousy player. Will was making a complete fool out of me in front of the other players on the team. The only reason I'd made the team in the first place was because he thought my sisters were good-looking. I flopped down on my stomach and was ready to head for the showers when it hit me. Elliot had come home. Lucky was gone, but Cerce was waiting for me. And Dr. Lewis confused me big time. I had no idea what all those things meant in the big picture of life, but in my small world they meant that I didn't need to give up because some stupid assistant basketball coach had it in for me. If he wanted to throw me off the team, he could. But I wasn't going to quit.

The rest of the team had already hit the showers at least ten minutes earlier when Will finally told me to take off. I stared at him for a minute before I followed his last set of instructions for the day. He didn't look like a mean guy. He didn't look like an angry guy. He didn't look like the kind of guy who couldn't get a girl if his life depended on it. He didn't even look like he hated me.

He was collecting balls when I turned around and instead of heading into the showers headed over to him. I wasn't sure what I was going to say to him, but I was trying desperately to come up with something strong and meaningful. Something that would show him he couldn't get rid of me that easily, that Benjy Morgan, younger brother of Jenny and Jillian Morgan, was a force to be reckoned with. Before I could get out one of those significant words, he turned around and noticed me approaching him. "You're getting there, Benjy old boy," he said. And then while I stood there, mute for a change, he smiled at me, gathered up the last ball, and left the gym.

Sixteen

I wasn't thinking about Amelia Parker as I rode my bike home. I was wishing that Peter would stop talking about what a jerk Will Sheridan had been at practice. "I wanted to throw the ball right into his mouth when he told you to hit the floor for that final set of push-ups," he said as he rode beside me. "He's nothing but a bully. I just don't know what he has against you. I mean, you're just as good a player as anybody on that team."

It was taking every bit of energy I had to make my feet pedal my bike. I had none left to begin a long discussion about the twins and the assistant coach. I was pretty amazed the twins hadn't told the whole world about the car wash scene, but obviously the word hadn't filtered down to Peter. Yet. "Beats me," I said, and let him rattle on about the practice and his two three-pointers and one near dunk.

We turned the corner to my street when I saw her

pacing the sidewalk in front of my house. Amelia was holding a white fluffy dog, and the look on her face was not the beautiful smile I saw when I closed my eyes at night. "So there you are!" she announced loudly when she saw me and Peter. "I've only been here for *two* hours! Where the heck were you?"

"We were at basketball practice," Peter said. He didn't even give me a chance to prove my muteness. He just jumped right in there and became my voice. "It was a terrible practice. Our assistant coach was wild. He . . ."

"I don't care what happened to *him* at some stupid practice," Amelia informed Peter, glaring at me as she spoke. "He was supposed to meet me right after school to bring Boo Boo to the shelter. What did he think I was going to do here for two hours? Sit on the step and listen to those stupid dogs barking inside?"

Suddenly I remembered Cerce, Jo-Jo, and Caesar. The poor dogs had been cooped up in the screened-in porch since eight in the morning. It was nearly five. It was surprising they weren't barking that loud, but I needed to let them out. I was trying to get off my bike very carefully, since every bone in my body ached, when Amelia grabbed my arm. "Where does *he* think he's going?" she asked Peter. "We've got to get to that miserable shelter before it's closed. My poor little puppy is going nuts here."

For the first time, I really noticed Boo Boo. He seemed like a pretty okay dog, just lying on the sidewalk, enjoying the last rays of the afternoon sun. Actually, that was exactly what I would have loved to do—sprawl across the sidewalk and let the sun bake my aching muscles. But I couldn't do that. I had three cooped-up greyhounds to attend to, plus one infuriated female, and a little dog that looked like a white mop. But there was even one more obstacle to my enjoying any pleasure whatsoever—the iron grip of Amelia Parker. That girl was one strong lady. I tried to unwrap her hand from my arm but she wasn't giving up easily.

"Tell him to get back on his bike and lead the way to the shelter!" she ordered Peter, who looked like her hand was around his throat. I couldn't believe it. Amelia's powers of making people mute had hit motormouth Peter. "Now!" It was weird having someone talk about you as if you couldn't speak. Or weren't there. It gave you a new freedom. I didn't mean to be a brute, but I had to get those dogs out of the house. I could hear them barking, and I knew they knew I was outside. Greyhounds are smart. Even though I hadn't spoken a word, all three of them knew I was outside. It wasn't easy, but I pushed Amelia's hand off my arm.

I should have been home free then. But I wasn't. Instead, I was attacked by a ball of white fur that dug its teeth into my ankle with such force that all the pain I'd endured in the basketball gym that afternoon faded away like a puff of smoke. This was pain, the kind that separated the men from the boys, and there was no doubt I was still a boy. I crumbled to the sidewalk, grabbing my ankle while Peter and Amelia struggled to get the white tiger with scissor-sharp teeth away from my foot.

"It's his own stupid fault!" Amelia was shouting. "Only an idiot attacks a dog's master in front of the dog. What did he expect? Look how upset he's got Boo Boo now! Poor Boo Boo." Somehow she managed to pull the beast from my ankle. "It's okay, baby," she cooed into his ear. The dog was baring his teeth and growling in his mistress's arms, anxious, I was certain, to finish the job she'd interrupted him in the midst of.

"Get that miserable dog out of here!" I shouted, my words silencing both Amelia and her vicious fluff ball. Truthfully, I was surprised I could speak, too, but more than surprised, I was angry. Angry that this girl, who was definitely the prettiest girl in our class, was talking about me as if I weren't present. Angry that this girl, whose beauty sealed my lips shut, didn't seem to care one bit that I was bleeding and in pain. Angry that this girl, about whom I'd been dreaming for nearly a year now, was keeping me away from three dogs who needed me a lot more than this nasty heap of white hair. "I wouldn't bring that dog to my mother's shelter if you paid me a million dollars," I told his owner. "Find him a home yourself. I don't care what happens to him."

"I can't believe how mean you are," Amelia said as tears fell down her cheeks. Man, was this turning out to be a nightmare. It was easy to yell at someone whose unrestrained dog was attacking me, but why did that someone have to start crying? "Boo Boo and I were nutty because we were here so long waiting for you. Do you know what it's like to be waiting for someone to take you to a shelter where they're going to take your dog away from you? It's torture. I'm sorry if you're hurt, Benjy, but you have to help me find a home for Boo Boo. You have to." The pathetic tears rolled down her cheek.

"He has to get his ankle cleaned up first," Peter told her, since I'd gone mute again, but he was free of Amelia's powers. Her tears had sealed up my vocal cords.

"That's the most important thing here now." Amelia didn't say a word as Peter helped me into the house.

The dogs were happy when they saw me, but the note attached to the back door explained why they weren't crazy wild. "The twins gave me the key to the back door and I got out of school early and walked the dogs," Wendy Brown had written on a piece of my mom's scrap paper. "I knew you had basketball practice after school. They're all great, but I might have to steal Cerce. Can you believe how much he looks like Lucky?" That girl was unbelievable.

While Peter led the three dogs into our fenced-in yard and threw a ball around with them, I cleaned up my ankle. It wasn't as bad as I'd thought. The dog had broken the skin, but it was a small teeth wound and one bandage covered it easily. "He's had all his shots," Amelia informed me when I walked back outside. "I can get his record from the vet if you want to see it." She was sitting on my front steps, holding Boo Boo in her lap and looking perfectly miserable. "Are you really not going to help me get Boo Boo into your mom's shelter?" she asked me, as if I were capable of speaking around her a second time. I nodded. "Does that mean you will or you won't help me?" she asked. I nodded again. "How about nodding once if it means you will help me and two times if it means you won't help me?" she suggested.

I felt like an idiot and a loser, but I nodded twice. She looked at me for a long time, and for a second I thought she just might sic her dog on me a second time. But she didn't. Instead, she stood up, holding her dog, which wasn't even growling, just staring nastily at me, and walked away. It would have been so much easier if she'd screamed at me again and called me names. I probably would have gotten my voice back if she'd done that. But she didn't. She was just like that miserable Dr. Lewis, making it impossible for me to hate her or her dog.

My mom was real quiet at dinner. The twins were psyched about some new kid who had moved into our neighborhood that afternoon. "I've never seen anyone so cute in my whole life," Jenny said.

"He's the most perfect guy I've ever seen," Jillian said. "Did you ever see eyes as blue as his?"

"He said hi to me at least three times," Jenny said. "I just love his voice. It's so sexy."

"When he asked me where I lived, I thought I was going to faint," Jillian said.

"He asked you where we lived?" Jenny asked. "I didn't hear him ask that."

"That's 'cause you'd already gone into the house," Jillian told her. "It was when I was walking Cerce and Jo-Jo for the second time. You'd already gone in with Caesar. Besides, he didn't ask where *we* lived. He asked where *I* lived."

"I can't believe you went out without me," Jenny said.

"You were on the phone with Billy," Jillian said. "I told you I was going out, but you ignored me."

"I didn't ignore you," Jenny said. "I didn't hear you. You obviously didn't ask me in a very loud voice."

"Girls, is there anything else we can talk about besides our new neighbor whose name neither of you seem to know and who may well be married with a family for all you know?" my father interrupted the two of them. "Something else must have happened to you both today besides this crucial event."

"I think I saw him when I was walking Cerce," I said. I wasn't the least bit ready for this conversation to die. But I knew why my father was. There was a definite feeling of hostility in the air. The twins, who hardly ever fought with one another over anything, preferring to concentrate all their hatred on me, looked ready to go at it with one another. It always amazed me that they got along so well. They each seemed to have this incredible sense about who got what, in regard to food, clothes, and boys. But this new neighbor had obviously awakened some sleeping feelings. They both liked him, and the first signs of jealousy I'd ever noticed between the two of them had come to life at our dinner table. Hallelujah.

"So have you heard anything more from Dr. Lewis?" my father asked my mother while the twins glared at one another and I excitedly watched them glare. The mention of Dr. Lewis's name, however, pulled me away from the twins.

My mother had ignored all the questions I'd thrown at her about Dr. Lewis when she got home from the shelter. I didn't even know if he'd come to see her at the shelter or not. From the minute she'd come home from the shelter, she'd been irritable and had prepared our supper with a telephone attached to her ear. The last person she'd wanted to speak to was me. "I told you he was supposed to call me by eight," she answered my father, sounding just as irritated with him as she'd been with me. I knew she was worried about Aunt Marcy. She'd gone to the hospital for her first treatment today and was supposed to come to our house for supper. But she'd been too tired after the treatment to do anything but go to bed. Uncle Bobby had decided to take Elliot out for supper rather than come to our house, and that had upset my mother.

As if by magic, as soon as my mother said those words, the phone rang. She jumped up to get it in the den. While my father and I stayed in the kitchen and listened to the twins snipe at each other, Mom talked on the phone for nearly an hour. By the time she came back, the table was all cleared up, the dishes washed and put away, and the twins weren't speaking to one another. It was an event I'd never witnessed before. The amazing thing was they were too angry with one another to pay any attention to me. They'd said nothing when I got more ice cream out of the refrigerator and didn't even comment on the scene during basketball practice, which I knew they'd seen. All I could hope was that this new neighbor wasn't married with a family and would never move away.

"I've got to go to New Hampshire now," my mother told my father when she came back into the kitchen. "It's very important I get there as soon as possible."

"I can't go with you," my father told her. "I'm on call through eight tomorrow morning and have a couple of tough patients to go back and see. Are you sure you can't wait till tomorrow morning? I'll cancel my office and drive you up then."

"Don't be silly, Mark," she told him. "I have no problem driving there myself. I do it all the time."

"But it's late and you're tired," he said. "I really wish you'd wait until morning."

"I'll go with her," I said. "I have no homework left."

"I might have to stay overnight," she said. "You can't miss school tomorrow."

"Why not?" I asked. "We're just going on a field trip to the Science Museum. I've been there a thousand times. Really. I'd like to go and see what's going on up there." The truth was I would have done anything to have avoided Amelia and basketball practice.

My mother looked at me and then at my father. He looked at me and then looked at her. And then it happened. He nodded. She nodded. "Let's get going right now," she told me. "Grab your book bag and some underwear and let's get out of here."

Seventeen

I couldn't believe Ellen's farm. The barn was completely burned down and a huge section of the field around it was scorched. You could still smell the smoke in the air. All I could think of when I looked at the blistered earth was Lucky. It hurt something terrible to gaze at the area. I wanted to close my eyes and turn my head away, but I couldn't do that. I owed it to Lucky to look, long and hard, at the spot where he, along with two other innocent greyhounds, had been so mercilessly murdered. I'm not a religious person, although I do make a lot of personal deals with God, but I found myself closing my eyes and uttering a little prayer to God to take care of Lucky and his friends and help me and my mom and Ellen find whoever was responsible for that terrible crime.

When I opened my eyes, I noticed for the first time that a new barn was already halfway up on a spot a short distance away from the burned-out structure. It appeared as if this barn would be even bigger than the one it was replacing. It was a miracle, I realized as I stared at the burned-out area again, that the main house hadn't been affected by the fire. I tried to calm the terrible aching feeling inside my chest by remembering what my mother had told me during our car ride. Dr. Lewis had spent several hours at her shelter talking to her about the fire. "Either the guy is the biggest liar in the whole world," she had explained as we drove to New Hampshire, "or he's had an abrupt personality change."

"It must be because of that Dr. Long," I had suggested. "She must have given him some human pills."

"Perhaps," my mother had agreed. "But it's all so hard to believe. This same man once chased me down five flights of stairs at his lab. If I hadn't been pulled forward by two lightning greyhounds, I would never have escaped from his clutches. He was a madman about his research animals. He despised me and my work to save the greyhounds. Now suddenly he's compassionate and sensitive about the animals. It's a bit much to accept. But your father claims it's believable. That Paul Lewis always cared about animals, but the research was more important to him. Now, however, Dr. Long has enabled him to do both, care about the animals and the research. The power of the love of a good woman is immeasurable."

That sure sounded like my father's words. But the rest of the story was harder to accept. Dr. Lewis had done some research of his own on the fire. He knew that my mother and Ellen suspected him of setting the fire and he was determined to do everything he could to find the real criminals. He'd learned that some guy,

George Arnold, who had worked for Ellen a few months earlier, had been in jail once. He was still trying to get some more information about him. Ellen had gotten really upset when my mother had called to tell her about the Arnold guy, and was going to find out whatever she could herself. It sounded as if the two of us were going to New Hampshire to keep an eye on the greyhounds and to help Ellen search out this George Arnold. All I knew was that both those deals sounded a lot more exciting than being tortured by Will Sheridan and Boo Boo Parker's mistress.

Ellen met us in the big house, surrounded by five greyhounds. Even though she had tons on her mind, she had made my favorite oatmeal chocolate chip cookies. The five greyhounds were beautiful combinations of brown and black with small sections of white around their faces and paws. Three of them were under a year and the other two weren't much older. They were all incredibly affectionate, and I sat on the floor, eating warm cookies and playing with all five dogs while my mother and Ellen got down to business.

"I can't believe George would do anything like this," Ellen told my mother. "He's the meekest man you've ever met. He's so small, probably one hundred twenty-five pounds soaking wet. His voice was so soft I could hardly hear him when he spoke. He never looked me in the eye when I talked to him. I gave up trying to shake his hand. It was way too hard for him to extend it in my direction. I felt bad when he left but truthfully I'd almost forgotten about him. He was just such an utterly forgettable man."

"So what exactly did he do for you?" my mom asked.

"All kinds of things," Ellen said. "He took care of the dogs and the chickens and livestock. He was a good worker. Not a great worker, but an adequate worker. He was only here for a year. Then, one day, probably six months ago, he just took off. He never told me he was leaving. He just left."

"Don't you think that was strange?" my mother asked. "You know, someone leaving without giving notice?"

"I guess so," Ellen said. "But I never thought about it that much. That was just the kind of man he was. You never really knew when he was here or when he was gone."

"But aren't you surprised to know he served time in jail?" my mother asked.

"Yeah," Ellen admitted. "He just doesn't seem like the kind of guy who could do anything wrong. It must have been for something stupid. Or a mistaken identity."

"Paul Lewis isn't sure exactly what it was," my mother said. "He has a friend on the Boston police force who's checking it out. He'll let us know what else they find out about him. But is there anything else you might remember about George?"

Ellen thought for a minute. Two of the dogs walked over to where she was sitting and put their heads in her lap. Nothing in this world is as sweet as a greyhound. For a moment it crossed my mind that I would have been much better off falling for a greyhound than for Amelia Parker, but I guess my father would have a ball with that particular thought.

"Well, there is one little thing," Ellen finally said. "He brought me flowers once. I mean, I think it was him. Someone left a bunch of really beautiful wildflowers on my kitchen table. I saw George leave the house that afternoon and he hardly ever came up to my house, so it must have been him. The funny thing is when I started to thank him for the flowers, he got even shyer than normal and looked like he was about to pass out. There was a note attached to the flowers that said, 'You're beautiful.' Weird, huh? Now that I think about it, that really was strange, wasn't it?''

"Sounds like he liked you," I offered from my spot on the floor. "Also sounds like a nut job."

"I agree," my mother said, shaking her head.

It was close to midnight when the three of us finished our talk and headed up to our rooms. I had just finished brushing my teeth when the phone rang. I walked into my mother's room when she was hanging up the phone. Ellen came in a few seconds later. "Unbelievable," my mother said. "Absolutely unbelievable."

"What's unbelievable?" I asked.

"That was Dr. Lewis," she said. "He found out what George was arrested for. Arson. He lit a fire in his high school when he was seventeen. The records were sealed but Paul got them opened. George was angry at a teacher for ignoring him. Apparently, he had a crush on her, but she never knew it. He spent six months in a youth detention facility for that crime. That was ten years ago and he's been okay since then. Still, it happened. No one was in the school, but he lit a fire there that caused serious damage. Paul's policeman friend has put out an all-points bulletin for him."

I've got to admit that it wasn't that easy getting to sleep that night. All I kept thinking as I lay in my bed was that Ellen's house was huge. And pretty far off the beaten track. It was in Concord, which is the capital of New Hampshire, but it wasn't in the nice downtown section. Actually, her farm was in the remote country section of Concord and the only building on this wicked long, narrow road. I'd always thought it was pretty neat that she lived so far away from other houses, but that night her farm's location didn't seem the least bit neat to me. All I could think about was that crazy George Arnold had very possibly burned down the barn and killed three greyhounds because Ellen hadn't thanked him properly for some flowers. Now, the only ones who were sleeping in this great big house were my mother, Ellen, five greyhounds, and me. When my mother suggested I take a shower before I went to bed, all I could visualize was the shower scene from *Psycho*.

A couple of hours later, when the rock crashed through my window and landed at the foot of my bed, I wasn't all that clean, but I also wasn't all that asleep. I had just been lying there, imagining someone coming into the room, looking for the bathroom with a five-inch knife in his right hand. I screamed. A lot less bravely than I would like to admit, but loud enough to bring my mother and Ellen and all five greyhounds racing into my room in about a minute.

The note attached to the rock was short and to the point. "You're beautiful," it read. "Too beautiful to waste your life on a bunch of stupid dogs."

"Oh, my God!" my mother shouted. "It's George Arnold!"

Ellen clutched the rock to her chest and shook her head. "I can't believe he's doing this to me. But don't worry. I'll go outside and talk to him. I'll get him to give himself up."

She was halfway out of my room when my mother caught up with her and tugged at her bathrobe. It looked pretty silly, my small mother trying to stop big Ellen from leaving the room. There was no way my mother had the strength to stop her from doing anything. "Please," my mother begged Ellen. "Don't even think about going out there. The man is crazy. Let's call the police right away." Still holding on to Ellen's bathrobe, she turned to me. "Call 911, Benjy," she ordered me, "and tell them to get the police out here right away."

Ellen stopped and faced my mother while I dialed as quickly as my fingers would move. It took me a few seconds to realize I wasn't hearing a dial tone. The line was dead. "It's dead," I informed my mother and Ellen. "Someone must have just cut it. I guess sometime after Dr. Lewis called around midnight. It's almost two now."

"Oh, brother," Ellen said. "Well, that's that. I have to go out and try and talk to him. He's half my size, Carol. I'll be fine. We have no choice."

My mother sank down upon the bed. "The guy is crazy," she said. "It's suicidal to go out there. Please, just wait a little while till we figure something out."

The truth was I was so scared I couldn't think straight. What I really wanted to do was to hide under the bed until the whole thing was over. But I was the only guy there. Even though I was only 12, still, I wasn't a baby, and I should be protecting the two women from the monster lurking around outside the farm with a can of kerosene and a book of matches in his hands. I should be the one who went out there to try and talk to George Arnold. I should be the one to sneak away from the house and run up the long, narrow

135

road until I got to civilization and could call the police. I should be grabbing a baseball bat and shielding these two females from the dangerous man about to turn us all into ashes. But I didn't do any of those things. Still, I did use my mind for one good purpose. "The greyhounds," I reminded the two women. "Where did they just go?"

Ellen jumped as if I had thrown a pot of water in her face. "Oh God!" she yelled. "They ran downstairs a few minutes ago. They probably heard something and went onto the porch. He could have gotten to them already."

The three of us raced downstairs but I was the first one to get to the porch. The screen door was open and the five dogs were gone. My mother slammed the door shut, but Ellen was right behind her. "I have no choice, Carol!" she yelled as she disappeared through the door and down the stairs into the cold black night. "I can't lose these babies, too."

"Oh, no," my mother moaned as she slammed the door shut again. "What are we going to do now, Benjy?"

I'd never seen my mother look so small and frightened. Even though I was practically her height, still she always seemed so tall and strong to me. After all, she was my mother. She could grab a hundred-pound husky by its collar and make it stop pawing me. She could say a few choice words and make my witchy sisters stop tormenting me. She could take one look at my most complicated math assignment and come up with the answer. My mother could do anything. But at that moment I saw that she was smaller and more frightened than I was, and that was one scary realization.

"I'm going out there," I told my mother, but those words made her smallness and fear disappear in one quick second.

"Oh, no you're not!" she said and the powerful squeeze on my arm convinced me my old mother had returned. It felt good to have her back.

"But we have to do something," I told her. "We can't just sit here and let poor Ellen get massacred by that sicko."

"I know," she agreed. "We have to do something, but I just don't know what."

Before the two of us could figure out what we would do, the smell of the smoke hit us. We looked out the window and saw the ball of fire at the end of the driveway. It didn't take either one of us long to decide what we had to do. We were out the door in a flash and racing into the woods beyond the house before either of us spoke a word. I wasn't thrilled to realize I was barefoot. And so was my mom. But that couldn't matter. What mattered was that we get out of that house before it burned down. The scariest thing was that we couldn't see any signs of Ellen or the greyhounds. All we could see was a ball of fire which was growing bigger by the second. If George didn't get us, his fire surely would.

Or else my miserable feet would. The rocks in the woods were killing them. My mother, I noticed, had already slowed down her fast pace. It would only be a matter of a few minutes before one of us had to stop. I never got a chance to see if my mother had more stamina than I did. Just when I thought I was going to collapse right there in the woods, I saw the car's head-lights coming at us from the end of the road. "Get off the road, Benjy!" my mother shrieked, but neither one of us was fast enough to get away from the approaching car. It was only when the car came to a screeching stop, inches from the two of us, that I saw the person sitting in its passenger seat. Never in my entire life have I been so glad to see my amazingly beautiful sister Jillian.

Eighteen

Jillian might have been in the passenger seat of the car that saved both my life and my mom's, but the driver was none other than Jimmy Oliver. Jimmy Oliver, who was thirteen years old and five feet eight inches tall, but minus a drivers' license. When my mother and I crawled into the backseat of the car beside Jenny, we were both too out of breath to say a word. My mom was the first one to catch her breath. "Drive as fast as you can to the end of the road," she ordered Jimmy, acting as if it were perfectly normal for an unlicensed thirteen-year-old to be saving our lives in the middle of the New Hampshire woods. "Stop at the first house we see so I can call the police and the fire department. Then we have to hightail it back to the house and find poor Ellen and the greyhounds. Hurry! For God's sake, step on it, Jimmy!"

I knew Jimmy could run like a rabbit and propel a skateboard like a flying whip, but I had no idea he could drive his dad's car like an Indianapolis racer. I also knew there had to be a logical explanation for how he and my two sisters got inside this car that made it to New Hampshire, but I wasn't all that curious to learn what it was. Not at that moment, anyhow. More important was getting the fire department and the police to Ellen's farm. It took what seemed like forever until we got to a house, woke up its inhabitants, convinced them we weren't escapees from an insane asylum, and used their phone to call the police and fire departments. Then my mother was behind the wheel of Jimmy's dad's car, and the neighbors were behind us in their pickup truck, and we were all barreling back down the road toward the farm.

As soon as the farm came into view, we could see that the fire wasn't blazing as much as before. As a matter of fact, the closer we got, we could make out a hose spraying water over the dwindling remains of the fire. "Ellen!" my mom screamed when Ellen's large frame came into clear view. "Dear God, it's Ellen!"

And sure enough that's who it was, holding the hose, surrounded by five greyhounds, putting out the fire. My mother put on the brakes so suddenly we would have fallen out of our seats if it hadn't been for our seat belts. It took another few seconds for all four of us to undo those belts and race to Ellen's side. My mother put her arms around Ellen, ignoring the cold water soaking her bathrobe. Man was I grateful that Ellen's house had been freezing that night and I had put on sweats before I'd gone to bed, or I would have been racing around the countryside in my underwear. "Thank God you're okay!" my mom shouted at her friend, hugging her so fiercely Ellen nearly lost control of the hose and soaked all of us.

"I'm fine," Ellen told her calmly, continuing to spray water on the smoldering fire and staring at the rest of the contents of the two cars. "Hey, Jillian and Jenny. Fancy meeting you dolls here. You both look gorgeous! Who's your cute friend? And, Ann and Henry. I can't believe they dragged you two snoozers out of bed. But, listen, you all. George is in the house. He feels terrible about what he did and understands that he's going back to jail."

My mother didn't have a chance to say a word, which is too bad because I would have loved to have heard what she would have said to that announcement, because the fire engines and police cars came roaring down the road at full speed. For the next hour there was a great deal of confusion and excitement, but when the smoke finally cleared from the air and from our minds, everything was surprisingly easy to understand.

And it made some sort of sense. A little after midnight, my dad had been called to the hospital for an emergency. A few minutes after he left, Jillian and Jenny decided to call me and Mom and see what was going on in New Hampshire. We were supposed to have called home as soon as we got there, but with all the craziness about George Arnold and Paul Lewis, neither one of us remembered to do that. Jillian kept getting a busy signal, so she called an operator. When the phone company told her the phone was out of order, she panicked. She tried to reach Dad, but he was in the locked ward with a patient and his beeper wasn't on. She called Uncle Bobby and Aunt Marcy, but they were sleeping and had their answering machine on.

Then, like out of a movie plot, Jimmy called, apologizing for calling so late, but wanting to speak to me. Jimmy's like that. He only sleeps a few hours a night and often forgets that, especially on week nights, the rest of us go to bed before midnight. The minute Jillian heard Jimmy's voice she told him how worried she was about me and Mom and the next thing she knew, he was pulling up to our front door in his father's Toyota. Mr. Oliver had come home at eleven-thirty from the gas station where he works the late shift and gone right to bed. Jimmy's mom moved out on the two of them a year ago. When she left, nothing seemed the least bit different in Jimmy's life. Apparently Jimmy had been driving without his dad's knowledge for over a year now and even had some experience on highways like the one leading to New Hampshire. "He's a terrific driver," Jenny said. "Better than you, Mom."

"Better than Dad," Jillian added. "He's fast, but not as fast as Dad."

"Weren't you nervous driving with someone who didn't have a license?" Ellen asked Jillian, staring intently at Jimmy, who was playing with the greyhounds, ignoring this whole discussion about him.

"Nope," Jenny answered. "We had to get to New Hampshire and it was either Jimmy or me or Jillian driving, so we chose Jimmy."

"Are you driving without a license, too?" my mom asked her. "You're just fifteen, for God's sake."

"Nope," Jillian answered. "Not at all. But we figured we'd learn real quick if we had to."

"Why didn't you go to Uncle Bobby's and ring his doorbell?" my mom asked Jillian. "He would have driven you here."

"We thought of that," Jenny answered. "If Jimmy hadn't come, we would definitely have gone there. But he came and we were out the door in less time than it would have taken to get over there and wake up that whole family."

My mom shook her head in disbelief. But Ellen's story was even more shocking. Sitting in her kitchen across from George Arnold, who had killed my favorite dog in the whole world, I wanted to feel enough hate to tear him from limb to limb. But I couldn't feel anything like that toward the pathetic, small man who sat there, sobbing into the napkins Ellen kept handing him. "He knows what he did was wrong," Ellen said, patting him on the back as if he were a sick child. "But he has a sickness. Well, two sicknesses. One sickness is that he gets crushes on people and doesn't know how to act toward these people. He has trouble expressing his emotions." George stopped crying for a minute and looked up at her and then dropped his head back into his napkin and continued his sobbing. "His second sickness has to do with fires. He lights them when his feelings get all bottled up inside of him and he doesn't know how else to react."

We might have heard a lot more about George Arnold's diseases if we hadn't been interrupted by another car arriving from Marblehead. This time the driver was my dad and the occupants were Uncle Bobby, Aunt Marcy, and Elliot. Aunt Marcy was the first one to reach us. "Thank God you're okay!" she yelled as she threw her arms around my mom. "I was worried sick when I woke up to get a drink of water and heard the message the twins left us. I called the Concord police and heard about the fire and called the hospital and got Mark, and fifteen minutes later the four of us were heading up 93.''

It wasn't long before my dad was hugging us all, too, and everyone was crying, especially George Arnold, who was sobbing more fiercely than ever when the police finally took him away. Ellen tried to convince them not to put handcuffs on him, but they wouldn't listen to her. ''You're as soft as a grape, lady,'' one of them told her, and I had to admit he might just be right.

Poor little Elliot looked like he was getting lost in the throng of huggers and police and firemen, but good old Jimmy came to his rescue again, making sure he got covered with kisses from the five greyhounds.

''Does this mean that all the greyhounds are safe now?'' he asked me as I sat down beside him on the wet grass and played with the dogs. ''No one's going to use them for experiments or burn them in fires?''

Man, did I want to answer yes. But I couldn't lie to my little buddy. ''No, it doesn't,'' I told him, sitting as close to him as I could. ''It just means that these five dogs are safe and that we're all going to work hard to make sure no dogs suffer needlessly.''

Elliot thought for a minute before he finally answered me. ''Mom says Cerce can come live with us,'' he told me. ''He'll be safe, right?''

''Absolutely,'' I told him.

It was light out by the time all three cars headed back to Marblehead. I was so exhausted I slept the whole way, squashed in the back between the twins. But they weren't vicious. They were almost nice. ''Will Sheridan called the house after you left,'' Jenny told me when I closed my eyes. ''He wanted to remind you about a

144

scrimmage or something with Medford tomorrow. Or today. That was nice, huh?''

"Sounds nice to me," Jillian said.

"You're not quitting or anything, are you?" Jimmy asked me.

I opened my eyes and smiled at him. "Why? Do you have something against quitters?"

He shook his head. "Quitting's not for everyone," he said. "Definitely not for you."

"Whatever you say, buddy," I said before I fell asleep thinking about one beautiful shot that sailed right into the backboard and fell effortlessly through the net. Man, was I sleek.

Nineteen

Everyone was standing around my desk when Peter and I walked into homeroom two days later. My mom and I had spent the day before at home, being interviewed by two television cameras and five newspapers. By the time I'd finally gone to bed that night, I was so sick of talking about the greyhounds and Ellen and George Arnold that I thought I was going to throw up. I'd also thought it was a good idea if I stayed home one more day to catch up on my sleep and homework and give my mouth a rest. But my mom vetoed that idea. "Everyone of us has twenty-four hours of being famous in our lifetime," she'd told me when she'd woken me at six-thirty that morning. "Yours is about to begin. Get out of here and enjoy it. It'll be over before you know it."

I wasn't thinking about being famous when I walked into homeroom. I was thinking about being abused by Amelia Parker and Will Sheridan. Even an appearance on the *David Letterman Show,* I was certain, would not prevent the two of them from figuring out some way to make my life miserable.

Amelia Parker was not, however, part of the large group surrounding my desk. Neither was Wendy Brown. But my mom had been absolutely right. I was in the midst of my twenty-four hours of being famous. Everyone, including kids who had never talked to me before, kept coming up to me all morning long, asking me questions, patting me on the back, shaking my hand, and telling me what a hero I was. I'd almost begun to believe them when Amelia found me. I was on my way to lunch. "I'm glad you and your mother saved the dogs you like," she snarled sarcastically. "Too bad lhasa apsos aren't as important to you big dog lovers as greyhounds. Thanks to you, Boo Boo's gone."

It killed me to admit it, but the girl, even with the hate in her eyes, was still the prettiest girl in our entire school. I sighed and shrugged my shoulders. I saw the group of kids approaching the two of us. I had maybe twenty seconds to say something. "I'm sorry," I said. Words were really coming out of my voice. I felt like the sensation at a prayer meeting. "The kid can talk!" everyone at the revival should be shouting. "Praise the Lord! The mute can speak! Hallelujah!"

"I'm sorry Boo Boo had to be put to sleep," I continued in this miracle voice of mine. "But the truth is he had a vicious streak. He shouldn't be allowed to terrorize people. It was for the best."

When Amelia's hand approached my cheek, I thought she was going to begin to kiss me. For a second my heart nearly stopped beating. I'd never kissed a girl in my whole life. I just hoped my cheek would know what

147

to do when her lips approached it. The smack against my face hurt so much I nearly fell backward. "You miserable creep!" Amelia shrieked at me. "He's not dead! He's at my aunt Denise's. I'd rather see *you* put to sleep than that beautiful dog." When she pulled her hand away from my face and stood in front of me, waiting either for me to speak or to slap me again, I noticed something amazing. Amelia Parker looked real ugly when she was slapping people. Her face got all red and blotchy and her black eyes got real little and squinty. And her nose seemed a lot bigger than it was when she was smiling at you. She just wasn't a good-looking slapper. I don't know exactly why I started laughing but when I did, she got blotchier and squintier and more big-nosed. Then she turned on her heel, tossed her hair back so hard it whipped against my face, and scrambled away from me as fast as she could.

"Hey, you okay?" Wendy Brown asked as she walked up to me, sort of edging out the crowd behind her. She was wearing her purple greyhound sweatshirt, the one that read SAVE A GREYHOUND AND WIN THE BIG RACE. "I think you just found the one person in the entire school who doesn't think you're a super hero."

"Oh, I don't think she's the only one," I said as we walked together into the cafeteria. "There's Coach Murray, too, you know."

"Well, I hope you're not going to let him slap you around, too," she said.

"Then I better quit, huh?" I said. It was real nice being a hero, but I knew my twenty-four hours were fast drawing to a close. My mother had already given me her basketball advice during breakfast, and as always it came back to my college application: "Quit the stupid team. It's not worth the aggravation. Besides, it'll look better when you apply to college if you join the newspaper." I was in the sixth grade and my mother was worrying about my college applications. Unbelievable.

My father had been equally as helpful the night before. "Decisions like this are never easy, Benjy," he'd told me as I was brushing my teeth before going to bed. "You're the only one who can decide if being on the basketball team is worth dealing with someone like Will Sheridan. I don't like to encourage you to quit something you want to do just because someone is making your path unpleasant. If the pain outweighs the pleasure, get out. But no matter what, remember: The decision is yours. No one's throwing you off the team. You're in charge here." As always, my father's advice left me staring blankly at him. For once I would have liked him to have said something simple like, "Don't let an idiot like Will throw you off the team," or "You'll never be able to play with a jerk like Will for an assistant coach, so get out of there." But I understood as I rinsed out my mouth, my father never talked like that.

My sister, however, did. "I'd never let someone make chopped liver out of me," Jillian had told me before she'd left for school that morning, even though I hadn't asked her opinion. "Tell him what you think of him and then throw your jersey in his fat face."

"No way," Jenny said, surprising me once again with her newfound ability to disagree with her twin. "Stay and sneer at him, and let him know you're tougher than he is. I'd die before I'd give that fat pant load the satisfaction of pushing me off the team."

It was Elliot, however, who had given me the best advice in our family. He'd called just before I left for

149

school to tell me he'd be coming over to get Cerce as soon as his dad got home from work. "Great," I'd said.

"Will you be there or will you be at basketball practice?" he'd asked, and for the umpteenth time I'd gotten that weird feeling that this kid just couldn't be five years old.

"I don't know," I'd told him honestly.

"I'll come cheer for you," he'd said, "if you stay on the team."

"I probably won't play during any real games," I'd told him. "I'll be a bench warmer every game."

"Oh," Elliot had said. "That's okay. Lots of Celtic players sit on the bench every game. My dad says they all help out in practice and it makes the team feel good they're on the bench. Waiting, in case someone needs them."

I'd thought about Elliot's advice on the way to school and realized that if I could face being a bench warmer, I would stay on the team. If I couldn't, I'd have to leave. I also tried to make another bargain with God. I asked Him to give me a sign about what I should do. If He thought I should stay on the team, He could maybe make it start to rain that day. If it got the least bit sunny, I'd quit. But so far the day had remained cloudy, not really raining and not really sunny. There was no doubt I was definitely losing my touch at making these bargains with God.

"So what do you think I should do?" I asked Wendy as she opened her container of cottage cheese and pineapple. Man, did that look like a lousy lunch.

She shrugged and dug her spoon into the cottage cheese. "I don't know," she said. "Play if you want. Don't, if you don't want to."

I opened my lunch bag and pulled out the tuna fish sandwich my mom had made me. Suddenly I was starved. "Thanks," I said to Wendy as I bit into my sandwich. It tasted incredibly delicious, with tons of celery and pickles mixed in, smeared with lots of mayo. Just the way I loved it.

Wendy stopped eating and looked at me. "For what?" she asked.

I'm not sure what I would have answered her if I'd had the chance to say a word before a group of kids I barely knew came barreling over to our table to join us. "Hey, how's the greyhound hero?" one of the guys asked me. Then his eyes landed on Wendy's sweatshirt. "Cool sweatshirt," he said. "Hey, are you his assistant greyhound saver or something?"

"Yeah, that's me," Wendy answered him, laughing. "Benjy's assistant greyhound saver. Just call me Mary Long."

I nodded and ate away, laughing pretty loudly myself. Dr. Lewis had Mary Long, and I guess I sort of had Wendy. Maybe, if the four of us were very lucky, we could fix things so no dog or person ever had to suffer needlessly. Dogs could be free from experimentation and people could be free from diseases like breast cancer. It sounded like a pretty tall order for a person who still didn't know if he was going to basketball practice or not. Still, I finished my delicious sandwich and bag of chips and four oatmeal chocolate chip cookies and container of chocolate milk and tried to enjoy my twenty-four hours of fame. I'd play if I wanted to. Or not play if I didn't want to. What could be easier? Except for loving a greyhound, I couldn't think of one single thing.

GREYHOUND ADOPTION INFORMATION

It is admirable to want to "save" an ex-racer, but adoption should not be done impulsively. Prospective owners should read up on the breed. The better adoption organizations screen greyhounds to provide a good match between dog and owner, provide information and veterinary care, including spaying/neutering, and are willing to provide post-adoption counseling when necessary. In 1996, more than 16,000 greyhounds found new homes through the dedication of hundreds of volunteers working with more than 200 adoption programs in the United States, Canada, and Great Britain.

If you are considering adopting a greyhound, contact the following organizations:

The Greyhound Project, Inc.	617-527-8843
Greyhound Pets of America	800-366-1472
The National Greyhound Adoption Network	800-4-hounds

IF YOU DARE TO BE SCARED...
READ SPINETINGLERS!

by M.T. COFFIN